It's All in the Mind

The Adventures of Walter J. Lodge, Thought Detective

Other books by Carl Japikse:

The Tao of Meow
The Ruby Cat of Waldo Japussy
Love Virtue
The Fabled Gate
Making the Right Things Happen
Exploring the Tarot
The Tarot Journal
The Hour Glass
The $1.98 Cookbook
The Zen of Farting

Fart Proudly (editor)
Poems of Light (editor)
Sophy (editor)
The Sinew of America (editor)

with Robert R. Leichtman, M.D.:

Active Meditation
Forces of the Zodiac
The Art of Living (5 volumes)
The Life of Spirit (5 volumes)
I Ching On Line (4 volumes)
The Light of Learning
The Revelation of Light

It's All in the Mind

The Adventures
of Walter J. Lodge,
Thought Detective

Fourteen mysteries
by Carl Japikse

Enthea Press ↪ Atlanta, Georgia

IT'S ALL IN THE MIND
Copyright © 2001 by Carl Japikse

All Rights Reserved. No part of this book may be used or reproduced in any manner without written permission, except in the form of brief quotations embodied in a review or article. Printed in the United States of America. Direct inquiries to: Enthea Press, P.O. Box 297, Marble Hill, GA 30148.

ISBN: 0-89804-856-7

Table of Contents

The True Blue Snafu 6

The Shootist 27

Meet Me At Chelsea & Main 46

The Woman in Blue 64

The Brush Off 81

The Night Nothing Happened 98

Thanksgiving 106

An Overture To Death 120

An Overdose of Bad History 134

Miranda's Rights 148

Gypsies! 165

Murder by Proxy 187

A Lot at Stake 203

The Needle in the Haystack 224

One

The True Blue Snafu

The man in the burgundy leather chair shoved aside a stack of papers he had been examining and, leaning forward, extracted a business card from a drawer. He slid it across the desktop to me. As I reached out to pick up the card, I noted a faint odor of crabapple blossoms in the air, but I assumed it came from some kind of cheap air freshener. It was just one of numerous false assumptions I would make that day.

"This should answer your question, Mr. Morgan," he said.

"I go by the name of 'Morgan,' sir," I replied. "I might not pay any attention if you call me *Mister Morgan.*"

The man chuckled, acknowledging my request with an indulgent smile. I picked up his card and read:

"Walter J. Lodge, Thought Detective."

Hmm, I thought—this fellow believes he is some kind of Sherlock Holmes. But I kept my opinion to myself—or so I thought.

Lodge looked at me inquisitively, as though

wall. "No, I am not Sherlock Holmes—Morgan," he announced, catching me completely off guard. "I am not anything like Sherlock Holmes. I am a thought detective. I do not investigate crime scenes; I do not engage in fisticuffs. I have no idea how to use a gun. I track crimes with my mind, nothing else."

"That's amazing," I spluttered. "You actually read my mind!"

"What's amazing about it?" Lodge asked. "Your mind is not much different than anyone else's. Which is to say, it is an open book that can be read with scarcely a miss."

I had arrived at the office of Walter J. Lodge with a confident air, perhaps even a trace of smugness. I had no idea who this Mr. Lodge was, but I had been sent to him with the highest recommendation by the Right Honorable Jack Steele, the mayor of our city. I had been told that Lodge needed a private secretary, one with some skills in police work. Having been assigned to the military police while in the army, and having worked as a press secretary for one of the mayor's political colleagues, I had been picked as the obvious choice. The mayor's confidence in me—and his glowing estimation of Lodge—had been more than enough for me.

But now I was beginning to have second thoughts. Lodge, I assumed, was busy having first thoughts. I was wrong, of course—but that was just something to which I would have to accustom myself.

"You'll do," Lodge proclaimed abruptly, then went back to his papers, leaving me sitting there.

"I beg your pardon," I asked. "I'll do what?"

"Quite nicely," Lodge said, looking up. This time I met the penetrating focus in his steel-blue eyes. For a moment, I almost thought his stare had engulfed my whole being, all the way from its essence to each cell in the physical body. It was as though he were weighing every atom of my character just as an assayer might evaluate a gold-flecked nugget. In the next moment, however, the sensation had evaporated.

Then Lodge blinked his eyes and laughed, realizing that I was not as adept as he at reading minds. In fact, I was not adept at all.

"I need a private secretary, someone with the utmost discretion. The work I do is of a highly sensitive nature, often involving the most delicate issues. As my secretary, you will assist me in many different ways—some of them quite ordinary, some rather bizarre."

"Bizarre?" I asked.

"Uncommon," Lodge explained. "This is why I need someone with police training. Your experience as an MP will be invaluable. You see, there will be times when I will have to rely on you to represent me in our work."

"Just what is 'our' work?" I asked.

"Crime detection," Lodge replied. "Only I do not use ordinary police methods. I use only my mental skills—the skills of thought detection—to discover the perpetrator and bring him or her to justice."

"If you just use your mind," I asked, "what do you need me for? I do not see how I can help."

"It is my firm policy not to involve myself in situations that might lead to actual physical harm—particularly to myself. In recent months, however, some of my cases have come perilously close to requiring my participation, and it has been awkward to bring them satisfactorily to a close. Had I had a fellow such as yourself to rely on to bring the action to its necessary conclusion, my life would have been much more tranquil."

At just over six feet in height, Lodge looked as though he could probably defend himself. In fact, he looked fit enough to knock a hand ball around a court with the best of us. He also seemed to be the very picture of poise and tranquillity. I could not imagine him frightened or alarmed—and still cannot.

"How does the mayor figure in all this?" I asked, more certain in my doubt than ever before. It sounded as if I was to be a glorified bodyguard—and I considered myself overqualified for the position. How wrong I was!

"Jack is my point of contact with the world at large," Lodge explained. "Until a few years ago, I had never bent my mental talents to any form of crime detection. I spent most of my time in pursuit of a greater understanding of the mind and its abilities. I consulted occasionally with medical doctors and psychiatrists, helping them understand the hidden implications of their most puzzling cases, but for the most part, I was left alone, ignored by the world and free to pursue any avenue of research that I chose.

"This blissful isolation ended when I helped a young patient recover from what appeared to be incurable leukemia. I did very little, actually. The child was already on the road to recovery; all I did was accelerate the healing.

"The child turned out to be the nephew of the mayor—his god child. When he heard what had happened, or at least what the doctors described as happening, Jack insisted on coming to meet me, to thank me personally.

"Even before Jack walked into my office, I knew he was a rare individual who could operate on compatible wavelengths with me. That is not to say that the mayor is intuitive himself in any appreciable way—intuition would be a terrible liability for someone in public office, especially someone aspiring to higher duties. I just mean that we communicated easily, without misunderstanding. It was as though we had been friends for thousands of years—which, of course, we had."

I gulped, not quite sure what to make of that statement. Lodge ignored my confusion, and went right on with his narrative:

"Soon, we were discussing the possibilities of using thought detection in nonmedical applications. As you might expect, His Honor was most particularly interested in ways it could help him become a more effective public servant. I was not sure that I shared his enthusiasm. But he was not to be daunted.

" 'I need your help,' he confessed. "You may be able to save my career, just as you have saved the life of my nephew.'"

"I was surprised by what I interpreted to be hyperbole, but as Jack continued to talk, I realized he was being completely serious—and realistic. His political career was indeed being threatened—by a scandal that had started many years before he was elected. But unless it was the mayor himself who exposed the scandal and cleaned house, he was apt to be brought down with it."

"Was this the True Blue Snafu?" I asked, using the term coined by the press after the scandal had broken.

"Ah, so you know about it!" Lodge exclaimed. "How excellent! You come to me not only with skills, but with knowledge as well!"

"I like to keep abreast of current affairs, sir," I replied quietly.

Lodge relaxed ever so slightly—a gesture that I interpreted as a sign that he was gaining confidence in me. "I should have known Jack would not send me anyone unqualified—or even uninformed," Lodge added, not so much with a tone of amazement as with a benison of approval. "What do you know about the True Blue Snafu?"

"Only the bare facts as reported in the press, I am afraid," I replied. "As I remember it, whole departments of the city infrastructure had been taken over by organized crime, who were using city government itself as a drug distribution network. Most of the deliveries were being run through weekly trash pickup routes—"The Stash Was in the Trash" was one of the headlines, as I recall. But both the police and fire departments—the men and women in blue—were used for deliveries and pickups as well, especially if any risk was involved.

"The whole scheme was set up by the former mayor, who continued to run it after being defeated. As I recall it, the former mayor testified in court that he thought the current mayor—our mutual friend Jack—could be kept in the dark about the drug operation for a long time, perhaps even his whole term. But I do not remember exactly what snafu led to the exposure of the ring."

"Of course not," boomed in Lodge, now almost eager to take up the threads of the story. "It was never reported in the press—they still do not know what actually happened even to this day. They are too busy chasing rumors and gossip to be able to recognize a fact if it hit them broadside.

"In my files, I call it the 'Augean Cleansing,' rather than the True Blue Snafu," he added, almost as an afterthought.

I stared at him blankly, failing to catch the allusion. Later, when I had a chance, I looked it up. Heracles, the hero of many ancient Greek myths, cleansed the Augean stables of centuries of dirt and filth by diverting a river to flow through the great structure. To Lodge, apparently, the mayor's dilemma was actually a grand opportunity to cleanse corruption from the city infrastructure.

At that moment, I realized I was going to have to expand the scope of my limited education a great deal to be able to work with a man like Lodge. Many years later, I suddenly realized that Lodge could easily have told me the meaning of his allusion himself. He just wanted to see if I would take the initiative to look it up—and then to continue expanding my mind in other ways as well. I was pleased that I passed the test.

Lodge continued telling the tale. "Like all people with criminal minds, the blue crew did themselves in. They began to worry that Jack would stumble upon their operation and blow the whistle on them. So they concocted a scheme to frame his honor as the original mastermind, if he ever began to suspect them. They figured that they could blackmail him—or, failing that, leave him holding the bag for their actions. Toward this end, they forged various documents which clearly implicated him.

"No one of any position of responsibility actually did this dirty work, of course—so that they could deny in court that they had ever been involved in creating the false documents. The actual labor was delegated to trusted lieutenants. But one of them took his assignment one degree too seriously—he not only forged certain incriminating documents, but had them registered officially through the office of the city recorder.

"One day, a friend of the mayor sent a courier to deliver some routine paperwork to the recorder's office, and happened to be handed the wrong file back by accident. Of course, I know that it was not an accident at all—nothing random ever occurs in this universe; it was an act of divine justice. Without knowing what the file contained, the fellow carried the folder back to his boss, who discovered the counterfeit document. Smelling corruption, he immediately called the mayor."

It was my turn to do the unexpected, as an old memory arose from my subconscious. With a gasp, I dropped my coffee mug, spilling the liquefied beans of Juan Valdez all over Lodge's Oriental carpet.

"Y-y-you are not going to believe this," I stuttered.

"I believe it already," Lodge confirmed, "but you are quite right; I did not anticipate it."

"I think I was the one who picked up the folder at the recorder's office!"

"You were."

"But that was four years ago!" I exclaimed, somewhat incredulously.

"Exactly!" agreed Lodge, coming around the desk to help me clean up the mess I had made.

"I am so sorry," I muttered, damning myself for being clumsy.

"Think nothing of it," purred Lodge. "You helped the mayor clean up a mess four years ago; the least I can do is help you clean up this mess today!" And we both laughed.

"But why did my boss never tell me what was in the folder?"

"Jack specifically asked him to stay silent about it. He wanted to wait until the time was right. Of course, he didn't have a clue what to do, but he knew he must wait—wait until he could gain the upper hand. So he did just that. He waited until the day he met me."

Lodge mused a moment silently. "Yes, you will do quite well. You see, you were already working for me four years ago, and we had not even met. In fact, Jack and I had not even met."

"Surely that was just a strange coincidence," I suggested.

"There are no accidents, and there are no coincidences," Lodge said with unexpected authority, almost as though the voice of God was speaking through him. In retrospect, I suppose that must be an exaggeration, but it seemed that way to me at the time. At the very least, he spoke with utmost conviction, a conviction that extended to powerful, incomprehensible depths and possibilities. "You were chosen deliberately to be the one who picked up the folder—I can see that now."

"Chosen by whom?" I inquired.

"Life. Divine justice, I suppose. It doesn't matter," Lodge said without further clarification. "But it would seem that I owe you some back pay!"

I am sure Lodge meant exactly what he said, but the back pay never materialized—at least in the form of an extra paycheck.

"The mayor knew, of course, that the document was a forgery, and so initiated an investigation which turned up other, similar papers. He knew he was being set up by people in his own administration—but he did not know why, or for what. It was at this point that he came to me—and I agreed to look into his problem."

"How exactly do you investigate a problem of this nature?" I asked.

"I think about it."

"That's all? How do you know what to think about?"

"There is always a starting point—the key that unlocks the latch on Pandora's box. In this case, it was the stack of forged documents the mayor had discovered, thanks to you. They still contained the personal vibrations of everyone who had touched them. It is as though every physical piece of paper has an invisible, mental counterpart filled with all kinds of valuable information—authorship, motive, and links to others. I was able to psychometrize the documents and focus on the person who had created them originally. My mental detection convinced me that it was a lieutenant in the police force. But it was clear to me, from reading the invisible essence of the documents, that the lieutenant was not acting alone.

"I called the mayor and asked him to come over. Which he did."

"And?"

"He was a little upset, because I had rather imperiously insisted that he leave an important fund-raising meeting. He was impatient at first, and clearly wanted to escape back to his meeting. But his attitude changed soon enough."

"How so?"

"I told him the author of the forged documents was a lieutenant in his own police department, male, age thirty-seven, a veteran of eleven years on the force. I suggested that the man in question was of Hispanic descent and loved to chew on lifesavers—to the point where it was an irritating nervous habit. I even opined that this nervous behavior was an outward expression of the inner conflict caused by the collision of Catholic guilt with his criminal actions.

"Suddenly, I knew I had commanded Jack's full attention. He had discarded his fund-raising mode and was focusing entirely on the issue at hand. 'Rodriguez,' he muttered. 'Jesus Rodriguez.'

" 'I beg your pardon?' I answered.

"The mayor looked me square in the eyes. "You have just described to a tee Lieutenant Jesus Maria Alvaro Rodriguez, an eleven-year veteran of the city's police force. Do you know this man?"

"'Only through this document,' I replied. 'To the trained mind, it is as good as a confession.'"

"'Hmmph!' snorted the mayor. 'I wish more judges sitting on the bench had a trained mind, then.' "

"I then proceeded to tell him that Rodriguez had not acted on his own, but was just a tiny corpuscle in a giant cancer that had infected the whole city government.

" 'These people are trying to set me up?' he asked at last. 'Why?'

" 'Why, indeed?' I parried. 'Because they want to frame you as the instigator of a massive drug operation they have been running through city hall the past six years.'

"The mayor looked genuinely stunned. 'How massive is massive?' he inquired.

" 'At least one hundred million a year.'

I let out a whistle of amazement.

"That's exactly how Jack reacted, too," Lodge added. "That worried me, because I knew the mayor was a man of great principle. He would want to round up the gang as quickly as possible. So I told him to do absolutely nothing until I gave him the signal.

" 'You are dealing with powerful enemies here, Jack,' I told him. 'Make sure that you do not make any false steps.'

" 'What can we do, then?' asked the mayor.

" 'I will set a sting,' I told him.

" 'Won't they suspect that?' asked the mayor.

" 'From you, of course. But not from me.'

Still, he had his reservations.

" 'Don't worry,' I laughed. 'Greed always gets the best of suspiciousness. Just remember: no matter what happens, do *not* get involved.'

Lodge laughed as he remembered the events. "What I did not bother to tell Jack, of course, was that I was deliberately planning to bungle the sting, so that I would be captured. I knew he would never let me go through with such a risky proposal. But I rather thought it would be a lot of fun.

"Needless to say, it ended up being a lot less fun than I had anticipated. Thugs are *not* pleasant people!"

He broke off his narrative and looked straight at me. The scent of crabapple grew stronger, but I still did not consciously pay any attention to it. "I survived my little scheme all right, as you can see, but halfway through, I was not sure I would. It was at that moment that the idea of hiring someone such as yourself first entered my mind."

"I would have been delighted to have joined you on that case," I assured my new employer.

"Well, it's a little late to put out the word when a number of pistols are staring you in the face."

I think I whistled again.

"I let it be known that I wanted to buy a large quantity of cocaine. I agreed to a rendevous with a number of men, all of whom were employees of the police department. Rodriguez was actually one of them. But I showed up without the required cash. Becoming suspicious, they seized me and hauled me off to a remote warehouse.

"As they were dragging me away, I decided to tear a page out of the play book of old Uncle Remus. 'Whatever you do, please do not let the mayor know anything about this,' I screamed.

"Rodriguez looked at me with an air of disdain. 'Why not?' he demanded.

" 'Because I am an old friend of the mayor, and I do not want this to reflect poorly upon him.'

"That was all the bait the blackmailers needed. Jack knew about my capture within the hour. He immediately took action to mobilize a rescue. Then he remembered my words: *'Whatever happens, do not get involved.'* Lodge paused a moment in reflection, almost as if he were amused by this point in the narrative. "Actually," he continued, "I almost had to hit him mentally with an invisible two by four to make him remember. He sat down as abruptly as he had leaped up. 'On second thought,' he mumbled, 'I don't owe him anything. Let it go.'

"Once we arrived at the warehouse, it became clear that they had brought me there only to kill me in an out-of-the-way, private place.

So I put the next phase of my plan into practice: I baited them."

"You baited them?" I asked, incredulous. "You taunted people who were intent on murdering you?"

"What better time to do it? They were already planning to kill me—how could I make the outcome any worse by taunting them?"

I shook my head in disbelief. "And what did you say to them?"

"It wasn't very pithy—nothing at all to do with their mothers," Lodge conceded. "I just said that they were wasting their time."

" 'Funny,' one of the gang responded. 'We were thinking about wasting you.'

"I laughed, just to show I appreciated his wit. 'You are bound to get caught,' I continued.

" 'Caught?' the loud-mouth continued, laughing. 'We have framed the mayor so well to take the hit for this racket that he will go down in history as the best-hung mayor ever.' He laughed at his crude joke—and so did I.

" 'You are framing the mayor?' I continued. "I would have thought that he was behind the whole operation. How could a scheme this big be going on without the blessings of the mayor?'

" 'The last mayor was in on it—in fact he

still runs it. But the current one—we haven't been able to get to him. But that doesn't mean we can't control him. We've set him up.'

"Rodriguez tried to shut up the loud mouth, but got nowhere. 'What does it matter what he hears? He's going to be dead in twenty minutes.'

"So we continued our banter for as long as I could keep the loud mouth talking. He managed to reveal almost every detail about the drug scheme—who was involved, how the deliveries were made, what kind of profit they made, where they got the drugs, and lots of other details. I continued to encourage him—and let the miniature tape recorder I had thoughtfully sequestered on my body record every detail."

"I was wondering about that. It sounds like you knew what you were doing," I interrupted.

"Not really—I could have used your help. But I had no intention of ever going it alone. The tape recorder was also broadcasting the voice to a patrol of state troopers, who by this time were camped outside, ready to swarm in, if I gave the signal."

"Did you?"

"Not really. When they were ready, they lined me up—I was trussed like a turkey about to be cooked—and they all pointed their pistols at me.

" 'May I ask one final favor?' I inquired.

" 'You can ask,' replied Rodriguez gruffly.

" 'Look in the chambers of your revolvers, and tell me what you see.'

"This request must have been odd enough to seem reasonable; in any event, they did.

" 'Hey!' cried the loud mouth. 'The chambers are empty!'

"The others verified the same was true for them.

" 'How on earth did you ever expect to kill me without bullets?' I asked, quite mischievously, I am afraid.

"Rodriguez did not take the bait. 'We can always just beat you to a pulp with the gun butts,' he said, advancing toward me.

" 'So true, so true,' I said. 'But you will have to do it without the ability to shoot back at the state troopers who are just outside the door, and are about to enter.'

"And enter they did, before anyone had a chance to lay a butt on me. They quickly handcuffed everyone assembled and led them off to jail. The rest of the gang was soon identified and apprehended, and the scheme had been busted. The rest is a matter of public record."

"That is amazing,' I said. "I have just one question. How were you able to remove the bullets from the chambers of the pistols?"

"Ah, that required a bit of magic, I am afraid—and a bit of luck. I did not actually remove any bullets from anyone's gun—the police record will confirm that the guns were loaded when they were confiscated. I used my mental ability to hypnotize the whole group into believing that they saw empty chambers when they inspected their guns. It is the kind of trick any good mentalist will perform night after night in his theater act."

"And the bit of luck?"

"That none of the untrue blue tried to use his gun anyway. The guns were still as deadly as ever—they had just lost faith in them.

"People are always making silly assumptions like that, I'm afraid. It's all in the mind, my dear Morgan—all in the mind."

Two

The Shootist

"Crime is one of humanity's most fascinating creations," Lodge remarked one morning while we were eating breakfast.

My work day for Lodge began at 7:30 at his mid-town home, when his housekeeper, a plump, good-hearted woman in her fifties named Molly Milledge, served breakfast.

Molly had been employed by Lodge for years, and was utterly devoted to him. I have no doubt that she would have laid down her life for him, if Fate had called upon her to do so—and she would have died happily. Fortunately, Fate only required her to cook our meals and manage the household.

Lodge had bought and refurbished an old estate, built in the early part of the twentieth century by one of the first men to market electrical appliances. He had no heirs, and when The Gentleman, as Lodge referred to him, died after a long, productive life, the estate was boarded up and left unused for years. Lodge was able to attain it for a most reasonable price.

"It was in remarkably good shape," Lodge

told me once—"not a bit of damage or theft from vandalism. One might almost think a cloak of invisibility had been draped over the whole property to protect it . . . if one didn't know any better."

"Perhaps it was invisible fencing," I quipped.

Lodge had brought the old estate up to date, but left the impressive art collection hanging on the walls, adding and subtracting only a few items to suit his taste. He also left intact much of the unique wiring and electrical gadgets that the original owner had installed for his own convenience and eccentricity. These included numerous devices that were years ahead of their time—remote controlled light switches and automatic timers, among others. One of the strangest inventions was a wiring system that transmitted all kinds of energy throughout the house in one wire—telephonic, electrical, even radio and television signals!

I once asked Lodge if he had ever had the art collection appraised. He nodded yes, saying that about ten years earlier it had been worth about eight million dollars. At that moment, a whiff of crabapple filled my nostrils and an image poured into my mind; I realized that Lodge had been using proceeds from a small part of his private art museum to pay his living expenses! When he took possession of the house, he had found many more pieces of art in storage. The ones he liked had been left hanging on the walls. But others had been set aside and discreetly marketed from time to time, bringing in a great deal of funds.

That impression was followed by yet another: a vivid sense that Lodge had been led to purchase the house by the spirit of The Gentleman! It seems he owed a substantial debt to Lodge for services rendered in an earlier life, and this was his way of "settling accounts."

The "vision," if you can call it that, disappeared as abruptly as it had arrived, along with the crabapple fragrance.

Lodge liked to read the morning paper with his eggs, dry toast, and coffee, and then outline the probable tasks of the day. It was not normal for him to dawdle over speculative conversation. Indeed, he would usually disappear after breakfast into his study to pursue his mental investigations, and I would be left with whatever correspondence or paperwork needed my attention. We would meet again at lunch and dinner. We often spent the evening in the Parlor—Lodge's word for the living room—and then we would each retire to our own domains—I to very commodious quarters Lodge provided me in the former carriage house, Molly to her apartment on the uppermost floor of the mansion, and Lodge to his rooms on the second floor.

Today, however, was starting out to be exceptional. Lodge was lingering.

"I beg your pardon?" I asked.

"Most people assume that crime is just a part of human life, but it was never designed as such. This is the only planet in the universe that has crime or anything like crime. And there wouldn't be any crime here either, if humanity could just see the truth about its own nature.

"Crime results from humanity's ignorance. It invents gunpowder, which gives humanity an explosive power, yet uses it to kill one another instead of building civilization. It invents dynamite, which lets humanity harness nature, yet uses it to blow up banks. It discovers nuclear power, which gives humanity nearly unlimited energy, yet uses it to destroy—or at least intimidate—nations. This abuse in turn engenders such massive fear that the peaceful generation of nuclear energy and the exploration of possible uses is restricted."

He turned and stared forcefully into my eyes, as he always did when he wanted an important idea to penetrate deeply into my consciousness. "Mark my words, Morgan; the failure of humanity to develop peaceful uses of nuclear energy is a sin of omission—one that will cause unnecessary suffering in about one hundred and fifty years, unless we mend our ways. The number of people who might die because we have failed to harness nuclear energy peacefully could easily exceed the number who have been killed by the bomb by more than a billion." He settled back into his chair, satisfied that he had punctuated his point.

"But crime is older than gunpowder or dynamite or nuclear energy," I observed.

"Well put, Morgan!" Lodge seemed almost pleased that I was following his discourse. "You have hit the TNT square on the blasting cap. These inventions have just intensified mankind's basic lust for crime.

"The moment a thinker realizes that human life is a closed system, the silliness of crime becomes obvious."

"What do you mean?"

Lodge stroked his chin. "In a closed system, nothing you do can disrupt the intended outcome. Anything you might do will be automatically balanced by the rest of the system, and will end up advancing the primal cause, even if only slightly. It is not possible to commit a crime against our system. Crime automatically engenders its own correction."

I still had no idea where he was heading.

"There are just two motives for crime," Lodge continued. "One is to acquire money or power or goods that are not rightfully yours. The second is passion. Would you agree?"

I nodded my head.

"So let's look at the first motive. Stealing money, or anything else, is just as pointless as handing out welfare. The thief does not learn to produce money in the process—just become devious. Once you retire from your life of crime in old age—or are retired before then by an unsympathetic justice system—you still have no talent. So crime does not enrich you in any way at all except in momentary wealth, which needs constant replenishment. The thief becomes a slave to his own inability to earn money responsibly."

"What if the thief steals a huge amount of money?" I asked. "Like four or five million dollars from a Brinks truck?"

"Only a truly stupid crook would ever pull a job of that magnitude," Lodge answered. "It guarantees that at least four sets of investigators will try to hunt him down: the police, the FBI, Brinks, and the insurance company. He will spend the rest of his predictably short life looking over his shoulder, hearing footsteps descend upon him. If a reward is offered, he will also have to elude bounty hunters.

"In addition to all that, even the successful theft of great gobs of money is fruitless. It gives the thief less motivation to develop a useful talent—beyond remaining undetected, of course.

"No, my friend, there is no job security in a large theft. It is much easier to prosper as a crook by making relatively small thefts. But in either case, the thief is trapped in a cycle of his own making, since life is a closed system. What is even worse—he will eventually have to repay every dime he has stolen."

"In most cases, that is not possible, is it?" I asked.

"Not in this lifetime, no," Lodge agreed. "But there are many ways that life can call in the accumulated debt.

"I was just reading in the paper an article about slave trade among Asiatic people. This is a particularly corrupt scheme: women in China who are trying to escape communism are induced to pay $40,000 in exchange for a new life in America. They are told they will be provided with passports, immigrant status, and a job. But when they actually arrive on liberty's shore, they are forced into prostitution and made to work for several years as slaves. When they are finally set free, they are still given no passports or status. They are illegal aliens in a culture they do not understand. Their only real choice is to go back voluntarily into prostitution.

"Throughout history, a lifetime in slavery has often been used as a quick way to pay off a large balance of earlier criminal activity."

"The second motive of crime is to inflict pain upon or kill someone you hate—or someone who has harmed you. But this is also pointless. By killing them or even hurting them, you guarantee the relationship will continue for thousands of years, in a seemingly endless spiral of murder and reprisal, lifetime after lifetime. This is not a matter of cosmic justice, as some might call it; by committing a murder or any crime, we magnetically imprint in our own character the need to atone for it. In essence, we automatically draw revenge upon ourself, somehow, sometime, somewhere. We cannot escape it, for we carry the mark of our crime with us—until we become a victim of our own transgressions, and learn how foolish we have been. Committing these crimes is hardly an intelligent approach to life."

Lodge stopped, looked up, and stared into space for several moments. His eyes were focused on a point far, far away. I began to smell familiar whiffs of crabapple. Then he turned to me. "Come, Morgan, we must go.

There is about to be an unfortunate incident at the high school. We need to be there."

We grabbed our coats and raced out the door. My car was the closest, so we took it, peeling out of the driveway and rushing over to the school. I drove. The school was less than a mile away.

"What's up?" I asked.

"That's what we are going to find out," Lodge replied. "I am afraid at least one student brought a number of weapons to school with the intent to do mischief. I just hope he hasn't started yet."

But he had. By the time we arrived at the school, it was already surrounded by police cars and ambulances. We parked and sought out the mayor, who had beat us to the scene.

"What are you doing here, Lodge?" Jack asked. "I don't think we'll need you on this one. It's pretty straightforward: a teenager went beserk and started shooting up the hallways. He managed to wound half a dozen kids, but we got here before he killed anyone."

"Nothing like this is ever straightforward," Lodge replied grimly. "I will not force my services on you, but I do suggest you let me poke my mind into this one for you."

"Be my guest," Jack replied with a shrug. "I think it's a waste of your time."

"Well," Lodge replied, "it's the only entry on my calendar today, so it would be a waste of time if I *didn't* take a look." And he strode off to walk around the school.

I was left without anything to do, so I wandered around trying to learn what I could. The lad had stood up in home room, screamed some kind of gibberish, and then began shooting. It seemed like a typical case of a kid cracking under adolescent pressures, but there was an odd twist. The kid had won numerous awards as an expert marksman; he could hit a moving bulls-eye dead center at fifty yards. But all of his victims were wounded; none killed. He had winged them in the left arm, missing the heart by only four or five inches. All six victims had been wounded in exactly the same way.

In late morning, the district attorney—an ambitious woman in her late thirties named Corinna Caxton—swooshed in from the court house, conferred briefly with Jack, and then announced that the lad would be arraigned for attempted murder and tried as an adult. The boy was facing a lifetime in a prison cell at the age of fifteen.

In talking with his classmates, I learned that the shootist was something of a conundrum. He had been a Boy Scout for three years, and was well on his way to earning his Eagle, when he suddenly dropped out of scouting a half year earlier. His friends said he was well-mannered and exceptionally helpful, but had seem preoccupied, perhaps troubled, in recent weeks.

"He just wasn't himself," one fellow told me, "but none of us ever expected him to do this. It isn't his style."

It was in late morning that the imported psychologists arrived, to help the kids who had not been shot—and their parents—deal with the pain and agony of the morning's drama. Even without Lodge's intuitive abilities, I could feel a wave of psychobabble descend upon the neighborhood, as the "experts" encouraged students and parents alike to get in touch with their grief and give in to sentimentality. There were a number of moments when I was sorely tempted to grab a gun and shoot the psychologists, but I remembered in time what Lodge had said. I certainly did not want to have to come back in a future life as a psychologist to compensate for murdering a few! Nothing would be worth that price.

It was late afternoon before any of us saw Lodge again. I do not know if he went home, or to the library, or just visited another planet—once he had disappeared around the back of the school building, no one saw him for hours. And then he was there, standing casually next to us—the mayor, the police chief, the district attorney, and me. One moment, he was not there; the next, he was. It was vintage Lodge.

"Well, Lodge," Jack inquired, "what did you find?"

"Just what I always find," Lodge replied. "The truth."

"That's what we've been looking for, too," chimed in the chief of police, an old friend of mine named Adam Goodman. Adam is one of those fellows who keeps a low profile in a large kind of way.

"I know, I know," said Lodge patiently. "But you always give up too soon."

"What does that mean?" asked Adam, a bit hotly.

"Truth is not something that can be discerned by physical evidence alone," Lodge said quietly. "There is other evidence to consult as well." He turned to Jack. "How are you charging the lad?"

The question was answered by District Attorney Caxton. "As an adult. Attempted murder. Assault with a deadly weapon."

"As I expected," said Lodge, shaking his head.

"What's wrong with that?" asked Corinna, a bit shrilly.

"Nothing at all—except that it would be a complete miscarriage of justice."

Ms. Caxton—she was one of those women who insisted on being addressed as 'miz'—threw up her hands in exasperation. "It's an open-and-shut case, for God's sake."

"More open than shut, I am afraid," Lodge countered. "Look—do what you think you must. But if you put this child on trial, I will have no choice but to testify on his behalf."

"What?" screamed Corinna, not bothering to camouflage a wounded look. "Why?"

"Because he deserves to be hailed as a hero. He was willing to give his own life to save the children he shot."

I have never seen three grown adults look more confused than the mayor, the police chief, and the district attorney did at that moment. But, I must confess, I was feeling a trifle confused myself.

"You had better explain yourself," said Jack.

"I intend to," said Lodge. "The gunman was a victim of black magic in an earlier life. He was not a willing participant, but he was a very passive person, and became a victim without much resistance. He had been an acolyte in the early Church, and was beginning to receive esoteric instructions. But his tutor was careless. The boy was kidnapped by evil men, and brainwashed to serve the dark path. He never did anything destructive while conscious, but he could be hypnotized and ordered to carry out all manner of unspeakable crimes and atrocities. He was a puppet, mentally and emotionally enslaved to his masters.

"In this life, he has been imprinted with a strong resolve—a steadfast determination, really—not to give in so passively to what others tell him to do. But the hypnotic link is still there. As he became a teenager, a war broke out within his conscience. Strong voices urged him to do all manner of nasty things, but he fought back with an equally strong determination not to violate his values and principles, or give in to the voices."

Lodge turned to the mayor. "Jack," he asked, "have you ever been standing on a bridge and heard a small, mocking voice in your head urging you to jump?"

Jack nodded yes; so did Chief Goodman and Ms. Caxton, even though they had not been asked.

"That's an inner voice of mischief, trying to lure you to your own destruction. You ignore it because you have strong values to the contrary and have no reason to follow such stupid advice. But imagine what might happen if you did not have a strong resolve that automatically rejects such gibberish. You might someday jump. And no one would ever know why.

"There are lots of strange things that happen inside peoples' heads, and modern psychology has very little understanding of them. The problems this young lad has been facing in recent months are way beyond the pale of ordinary criminal behavior.

"All this came to a head this morning. For the last two or three weeks, the voices in his head have been insisting that he take his guns to school and execute his classmates, or they would make his life hell for him. From what I can tell, they gave him ample samples of just what this hell would resemble. The kid suffered greatly from these demonstrations, but hung in there, refusing the demands of the voices.

Lodge paused a moment, then continued.

"We usually see this kind of pattern in fanatic religious leaders, where a paranoid leader of some fringe group convinces his followers that they must join him in mass suicide. These people never set out with murder in mind, but they become possessed and manipulated—and finally break down. It is odd that a fifteen-year-old lad would fit this profile, but we live in odd times.

"Finally, in desperation, he worked out a plan. He would take the guns to school, pretend to shoot a few kids, and then kill himself. He had decided that suicide was the only way he could murder the demonic voices that were controlling him. He viewed his plan as a form of sacrifice.

"It should be obvious that he never intended to kill anyone but himself. Would an expert sharpshooter miss six shots in exactly the same way? Of course not. He shot to protect the students from his violent rage, not kill them. Then he put the gun in his mouth and was about to shoot when his plan misfired."

"What happened?" asked Chief Goodman.

"You arrived," said Lodge quietly. "And the first officers on the scene disarmed the boy before he could kill himself. So he was unable to kill the voices within himself—and now he faces life in prison, alone with his fiendish tormentors."

"And how do you know this?" demanded Corinna. Jack shot her a withering look that commanded her not to insult Lodge with silly questions, but Lodge stepped in to prevent a stare-down.

"A fair question," Lodge answered serenely, "probably the first good question you have asked today. The boy told me."

"What?" chorused Corinna and Adam in unison. "He's been in my custody ever since the shooting," Chief Goodman continued. "How could you have possibly interviewed him?'

"It's all in the mind," Lodge said triumphantly. "Morgan here will confirm that we were just idly enjoying a chat over breakfast this morning when I suddenly became aware of a terrible tragedy at the high school. That is why we showed up without being summoned."

"That is true," I confirmed. "How did you know?"

"The shootist himself showed up, like an apparition, and pleaded for my help. He said that he was being forced against his will to shoot his school mates."

"How did he know to seek you out?" Jack asked.

"In this universe, the law of compassion is even stronger than the rule of law. He desperately needed help; the force of compassion drew him to the only one close enough to assist him. That is the way compassion acts.

"Of course, I did not get the full story in that initial moment. The lad was too confused. But there was no great difficulty in piecing the puzzle together after he was in custody. I made contact with him mentally through the link he had already created when he asked for help, and the story came out quickly enough."

"Why have you been missing for five hours then?" Jack asked.

"I wasn't going to report back to you until I had thoroughly verified what the boy told me," Lodge replied, slyly. "There are plenty of beings out there who love to play jokes on slightly intuitive but gullible people. I do not like to be fooled. I spent the rest of the time checking out his earlier lives and destiny in the Archives."

"The Archives?" asked the district attorney.

"That's what I call it," Lodge replied. "It's basically the collective memories of the human race."

"Why did he bother winging the six kids?" asked Chief Goodman. "Why didn't he just shoot himself at his house?"

"The nasty voices would never have let him get away with that," Lodge replied, as though he were repeating math problems to a group of slow pupils. "Keep in mind that they were present in the lad's mind; they knew what he was thinking and planning. So he had to concentrate very carefully not to tip off his true intentions, lest they prevent him from carrying it out. He did so by vividly imagining the pain he was going to inflict. This kept his tormentors distracted."

"Well," Jack interrupted. "We still have the problem of what to do. Public opinion will not let us discharge him and set him free. The boy would be lynched within forty-eight hours."

Lodge laid out his plan. "Ask the court to find him innocent due to criminal insanity, and then commit him to a proper psychiatric facility. I am sure his attorney will be happy to go along with any plan along these lines. I happen to know a quaint little nursing home run by a colleague of mine that would understand exactly how to treat him. Once he recovers from his trauma—which he will—he will be a fine young man.

"In fact, he has an important destiny to fulfill in about twenty years—under a new name and identity, of course. "

Three

Meet Me At Chelsea & Main

Lodge had been pulling my leg all morning. Standing next to the open window in his study, he had pretended to talk to an invisible bird—a bird that he claimed he had summoned from the ethers and would figure in our next case. I was still too much a novice in my work for him to know for sure whether he was serious or teasing me.

He would coo gently and then seem to stroke a bird in his hand. "It's name is Sylvia," he announced. "Sylvia comes to me from time to time; she is lonesome and seeks out my company."

"How could she be lonesome?" I asked. "It is clear that she is invisible, if in fact she exists. I am inclined to think you are just having a joke at my expense," I protested.

Lodge put on a long face and looked positively bereft, as if I had taken his most precious possession from him.

"How can you say such a thing?" he asked mournfully. "Look, you have hurt Sylvia's feelings." And he held out his hands as though he were showing me something I plainly could not see.

"Can you explain to me how something that does not exist can be hurt?" I asked, deciding to take up the joke.

"Because she sees the truth: that you do not believe that she exists," said Lodge. "You have hurt her concept of herself—the most precious thing that any living being can possess."

This last sentence should have been a red flag to me—I knew Lodge despised the current emphasis in education and social work on coddling the self-esteem of low achievers. But I failed to catch the tone of irony in his voice.

We continued in this vein of bantering for some time, until he took a new tack. "I shall prove she is real, even if she is invisible," Lodge declared. "I shall feed her." He left the sill and went over to a small dish setting on a nearby bookcase. It was filled with sunflower seeds. Lodge scooped up a handful and went back to the window, where he extended his hand. I watched with amazement while, one by one, the seeds disappeared from his hands.

I shook my head. "It's an impressive trick, I will grant you, Lodge, and I wish I knew how you did it. But I am not about to start believing in birds I cannot see."

"Aren't you a Catholic?" Lodge asked me, suddenly stern.

"You know that I am," I replied. "What does that have to do with birds I cannot see?"

"Are you not taught that the Holy Ghost often presents itself as a bird—specifically a dove?"

"Sure."

"Are you capable of seeing the Holy Ghost? Do you know anyone who can see the Holy Ghost?"

I confessed that the answer to both questions was "no."

"Then why are you so hasty about declaring that Sylvia does not exist? It seems to me that you should believe just the reverse. She is a dove, after all."

I shook my head and cried "uncle." I should have known better than to try to argue with Lodge, even in jest. But he was not ready to let it rest. "What is that you say, Sylvia?" he suddenly asked, as though cocking his ear to hear better. "The mayor is approaching and has a case for us?"

I groaned and sat back in my chair. "You can see the driveway from this window," I said. "If Jack is really approaching, you know it because you have seen his limo drive up—not because a bird that I cannot see told you!"

Lodge graciously accepted my rebuttal. "You are very observant, Morgan," he said. "It will be a long time before I can pull any wool over your well-trained eyes."

Moments later, our housekeeper, Molly Milledge, announced Jack Steele's arrival. As Lodge turned from the window to greet the mayor, His Honor asked: "Well, what'll it be, Lodge? Shall I tell you what brings me calling this morning, or shall you?"

"This time," Lodge replied, still chuckling, "why don't you tell me why you *think* you are here, and then perhaps I will tell you the real reason."

"That's why I keep coming," Jack muttered, shaking his head in mock frustration. He sat down. Lodge had settled into his own chair behind his desk. We formed an almost perfect equilateral triangle.

I noted, perhaps for the first time, that Jack was a rather imposing man. I mused on the fact that his surname was "Steele"—a man of steel, if not of iron. Somehow, in a fuzzy corner of my mind, I heard Lodge's voice elucidate on my musings: "Stele, not Steele—a pillar of strength among men." It was days later before I suddenly thought to look up the word *stele* in the dictionary. It refers to an inscribed stone pillar.

The mayor threw up his hands to emphasize his urgency. "The police have discovered a criminal cartel laundering tainted money through our city," he began. "Chief Goodman thinks there is a distribution network of about thirty runners, but the police have been unable to penetrate the operation. Every time we start to get close, they back off and restructure their operation. It is starting to get to be a real problem. I am becoming quite concerned. I hope you can help."

"I'll see what I can do," Lodge said pleasantly.

"That's it?" Jack asked, somewhat dumbfounded. "You'll see what you can do? That sounds as though you don't know what to do. Usually, you have the answer to my questions before I even finish asking them! I thought I would leave today with all the information I needed."

"Every case is unique," Lodge smiled. "Today your information is: 'I'll see what I can do.'"

"Oh," Jack replied. He was not disappointed, just confused. And then, a moment later, he brightened up. It was as though he had figured it out: Lodge knew, but had decided not to tell, for some reason known only to himself. "Well, when you have something for me, let me know."

"I shall," Lodge promised.

"I won't keep you any longer, then," Jack said, and left. Once the mayor was gone, Lodge turned to me and asked me to check the usual sources and leads.

"Isn't that what the police force is already doing?" I asked.

"I can't rely on their information," Lodge said. "I need your own personal investigation in this case."

"Well, can you give me a hint where to begin—perhaps a name—so I don't have to waste my time?" I asked.

"You'll get it when you need it," he replied. "In the meantime, don't worry about wasting time. You do it with the utmost professionalism." I never have decided if that was a compliment or not.

So I hit the streets. But the mayor was right—this gang was slick. Each time I started to close in on a lead, it evaporated in thin air. I spent days checking out tip after tip, only to end up at week's end with less information than I had when I started.

"All I can say for sure," I told Lodge when I reported back, "is that they operate out of Miami and have about five guys in the field here. They change their local base almost every day, to conceal their tracks. They pick up funds on a revolving schedule from drug dealers, prostitute rings, and bookies. I have seen them receive cash, but I have never been able to catch them delivering it. It's almost as if one of their pick ups is also their delivery point, but I cannot figure out which."

Lodge accepted my report without comment, except to say I was doing fine.

The next day being Saturday, I had the day off. I decided to do some shopping downtown, at a large department store. I was happily browsing through a mountain of shirts on sale when a voice sounded again in that remote corner of my mind.

"Morgan, I need you."

It sounded like Lodge. I looked around, expecting to see him next to me at the bargain shirt counter. He was not there. I instantly realized how foolish that notion had been: Lodge would never stoop to wearing a bargain shirt!

I went back to browsing. Once again the voice echoed in my mind:

"Morgan!"

This time, it was accompanied by the familiar faint trace of crabapple. It *was* Lodge!

Still, I was not ready to admit that I had telepathic rapport with my employer. "I must be hearing things," I muttered, and went back to shopping. I even tried to block out the voice in my head, as though it were a gnat buzzing about. Or perhaps a dove.

The third time, the voice sounded as clear as a bell.

"Morgan! You *are* hearing things. Specifically, *me*. If you can stop spending your money on poorly tailored shirts, I need you to meet me at the corner of Chelsea and Main. Please!"

With that, the fragrance of crabapple began to dissipate, and I knew that Lodge had concluded his transmission. I left the department store and hailed a cab to take me to Chelsea and Main. I was there within five minutes. But Lodge was not. He was nowhere to be seen.

I was not disturbed—yet. I reasoned that Lodge had not expected me to take the cab, and had thought that he could arrive at the appointed rendezvous in the same time I would require. So I waited.

The part of town where Chelsea intersects with Main is one of the most notorious districts in the city. Basically, the hookers who parade their wares on Chelsea buy drugs from the pushers who have taken over Main Street. Even though it was the middle of Saturday morning, the hustling on both streets had already begun—and business was being conducted quite openly. I tried to look as inconspicuous as possible; I was not in the habit of spending my Saturday mornings standing around on either Chelsea or Main.

Ten minutes passed, then twenty. Lodge was as invisible as that bird of his—and now inaudible as well. I worried that he must have been unaccountably delayed, and the whole plan he had worked out—whatever it was—would fall apart. I strained to see if I could get a mental impression as to what to do next, but to no avail. I had a strange sense that Lodge was close by, but that was all. The contact was broken, and I could not fix it.

About that time, a pigeon flew by. I began to daydream idly. Could it be—could it possibly be Sylvia? I rebuked myself for being so gullible. "There must be a hundred thousand pigeons in this town. This is *not* Sylvia. Sylvia does not exist."

I was following the flight of the bird, not paying attention to anything else, when I was rudely knocked to the ground by a *latino* who also was not paying attention. He muttered,*"Perdónome,"* helped me up, then hurried on his way. But in the moment it took him to help me up, I recognized that he was *El Gordo,* one of the primary figures suspected in the money laundering cartel. They called him *El*

Gordo because he was as thin as a straw and quick on his feet.

I forgot all about Chelsea, Main, and Sylvia and began following my prey. I nearly lost him a couple of times, but I managed to keep the trail, even though once it seemed to be only by divine intervention. I thought about the dove and gave credit—and thanks—to the Holy Ghost.

Finally, *El Gordo* darted into a building. I concealed myself in an alley and kept watch on the building. Two hours later, he and the rest of the members of the cartel emerged, got into a car, and sped away.

I returned to Lodge's estate. He was at the window, looking out.

"Where were you?" I asked Lodge, somewhat heatedly. "I waited for you almost half an hour at Chelsea and Main. You never showed up."

"I never claimed I would," Lodge said with a snicker. "I simply asked you to meet me at Chelsea and Main. Which you did. I am quite proud of you. You have confirmed all of my suspicions in this case."

"Since you weren't there, how do you know I showed up?" I asked.

Lodged beamed, as though he could not believe the opportunity I had just given him.

"Why, a little birdie told me so," he chortled.

I sat there and pouted. "Are you suggesting that you brainwashed me into doing what I did today?"

"Come, come, Morgan," he continued, "it wasn't brainwashing at all. If I had asked you man to man to trail *El Gordo,* you would not have hesitated to do so. What makes the difference if I communicated mentally instead of physically to you?"

"I didn't know what was going on," I said.

"Do you ever?" he asked. "Does Jack know what we have been doing today? Of course not. Yet he assumes we are working on the case, which we are. In fact, we have solved it. Is that fact diminished in any way because he is not consciously aware of what has been going on?

"Does anyone ever really know the inner implications or larger ramifications of what they are experiencing on earth? Very, very few. But that doesn't mean they are brainwashed.

"As I sat here this morning, I knew mentally that someone in the cartel would be hurrying through the intersection of Chelsea and Main in a very short time—and that you were only a cab ride away. I had waited a week for this opportunity—and I had made sure that you used the week as best you could to become familiar with the cartel's principals. As your path and his began to intersect, they formed an opportunity—the opportunity we needed. It may seem like a coincidence to you, but this is how life's intelligence solves problems—it creates opportunity. It is up to us to recognize and seize the opportunity.

"I knew you would be downtown all day, so I decided to contact you telepathically. This being your first real experience with telepathy, you ignored me twice. That is to be expected. It also proves that you could not be brainwashed—you rejected my contact. But you knew it was me—thanks to the crabapple—and you responded very well, receiving the message as transmitted.

"Once you arrived at Chelsea and Main, it was just a matter of making sure that you made contact with the right person. I did not actually have to intervene in any way; you handled this all by yourself, even though you did not know it. After a week on the case, you had built up such a strong intention to nab this gang that you actually drew the suspect directly to you, once he entered your range—and caused him to bump into you."

"Bump?" I repeated, sounding as wounded as I could. "He knocked me down!"

"I know," Lodge smiled. "And that gave you the opportunity to inspect him up close. You needed to make an absolutely positive identification."

"I did that," I sighed.

"And then you did what I could not have done," Lodge continued. "You used your police skills to trail him back to the cartel's headquarters. You have done what the whole police force could not do. Well done!"

I accepted his congratulations, but was still uneasy. "It seems to me that the plan depended an awful lot on luck."

"How so?" inquired Lodge.

"I almost lost him twice. The second time, he disappeared entirely. It was only a stroke of good luck that he reappeared moments later."

"Luck?" Lodge sniffed, as though he were insulted. "Luck? The alley where you lost him still stinks of skunk."

"Skunk?" I repeated. "I never saw a skunk."

"Of course not—nor smelled it, either. But the suspect did.

"Naturally, I did not expect you to lose him, even for a moment. When you did, I had to act quickly. The skunk was the best I could do. It wasn't a real one, of course—I cannot precipitate skunks out of the ether any more than doves. But *El Gordo* thought it was real—and it certainly smelled real. When *El Gordo* finally did make it to his headquarters, he had a very hard time explaining why he smelled so foully. It took him a whole hour to clean up before they could leave. In fact, it messed up a major drug deal that had been scheduled for today. His associates are presently quite furious with him."

"And that's not brainwashing?" I asked.

"Of course it is brainwashing," Lodge agreed amiably. "So what? The guy is a criminal. He preys upon the minds and lives of the innocent. If it is a sin to brainwash such a man, it must be a very, very small sin. *De minimis non curat lex*."

"What does that mean?" I asked.

"It's Latin. 'The law does not worry about trifles.' In this case, it is divine law." Lodge paused for a minute, and then added: "I think it is time you learned something very important about brainwashing."

"What's that?"

"No one can be brainwashed, even by me, unless they want it to happen," Lodge said.

"I'm not sure I understand," I said.

"Were you the only one at the sale this morning?" Lodge asked.

"Of course not," I replied. "The place was

packed. There's probably not a shirt left for me by now."

"Exactly. Probably a thousand thoughts were bombarding you at that sale table, most of them involving greed, possessiveness, and envy. Yet there was only one voice that you chose to respond to—mine. How could that be brainwashing? You ignored me twice before choosing to accept the message. If you were brainwashed, you did it to yourself."

"I see."

"Then, while you were waiting for me at Chelsea and Main—and I did meet you there, mentally—you were bombarded by hundreds of other thoughts. Hookers tried to tempt you, not just physically but also psychically. I've been to Chelsea; I've heard the incessant din. Thoughts of 'Buy me! Buy me!' are constantly bouncing off the buildings, streets, and vehicles. Some of it is even more explicit.

"Drug pushers also tried to seduce you. But you refused to be brainwashed. It is always your choice, don't you see?"

"So it was *El Gordo's* choice to believe in the skunk—and smell it?"

"Precisely. *El Gordo* is a very superstitious man, as so many people are. His own character reminded me of a skunk, so skunk it was. But I did not brainwash him. I reflected his own tendencies back to him—but he did the rest. He made the choice.

"In fact, if anyone brainwashed someone today, it was you."

"Me?"

"Yes, you—when you unknowingly drew *El Gordo* to you by the strength of your determination to break the case. That was a true magnetic example of brainwashing."

I knew he was right—but I didn't like it. I do not engage in brainwashing. I much prefer fisticuffs.

"So, what do we do next?" I asked.

"We call Jack and give him the information he requested. The police can handle raiding the headquarters and arresting the cartel."

"But what about evidence?" I asked. "Sure, I can identify *El Gordo* as the man who ran into me, but that does not prove his connection with a cartel."

"It doesn't?" Lodge asked, amused. "Why don't you look in your coat pocket? On the right side."

The coat was in the hall, hanging on an old fashioned coat rack. I reached into the pocket. I found a plastic bag. I opened the bag and poured out the contents. Currency. Lots of it. Mostly in five and ten dollar denominations.

"How did that get in my coat pocket?"

"The reason *El Gordo* was running in the first place," Lodge explained, acting like a plump little Belgian parsing out his secrets, "is because he began to believe that he had been spotted making a pick-up. He thought the police were hot on his heels, and wanted to dispose of the cash he had been collecting before he got caught. When he bumped into you, he saw his chance. He gave you his hand in order to help you up—but only so that he could slip the bag into your coat pocket!"

"Well, I'll be!" I said.

"Those are marked bills you have there, Morgan, substituted for the real cash by a police informant working at one of the pickup spots. I think we have all the evidence the police will need. It all came together just as surely as Chelsea intersects Main. You have done a good day's work, Morgan—an excellent day's work."

"Just one more question, Lodge."

"What?"

"The dove I happened to notice just before *El Gordo* ran into me—was that Sylvia?"

Lodge stopped and stared right through me as if he could not believe that I was solid. "Sylvia was just a joke, Morgan. You have to stop believing everything I say—especially the stuff you cannot see."

"But what about her eating out of your hand?" I asked.

"Didn't you say yourself that it was a trick?" Lodge replied.

"I did—but I didn't believe it, I guess," I responded.

"If you look at the floor by my window, you will see the sunflower seeds I let slip between my fingers," Lodge said, with almost a tone of pity in his voice.

"So the pigeon I saw wasn't the Holy Ghost?" I asked, disappointed.

"Absolutely not. It was all in your mind."

But was it? For the next several seconds, the room was flooded with the odor of crabapple—and if a scent could smile, this bouquet certainly did.

Then, in less than a moment, it all disappeared.

Four

The Woman in Blue

Great works of art hung in prominent places throughout Lodge's home, but one room—he called it the *"atelier"*—was special. It was a room in which only the art work of Jean-Honoré Fragonard was on display—some twelve canvases in all, many of them unknown to the art world. Fragó, as he was known by his contemporaries, had been a particular favorite of The Gentleman—the wealthy electrical genius who had built and occupied Lodge's estate originally. He had assembled his impressive collection of paintings by Fragonard before the artist's reputation had driven prices for his work into the stratosphere. The twelve paintings now owned by Lodge were, by themselves, worth a fortune.

Not that Lodge would think of selling them. For Lodge, the *atelier* was something of a holy place—a shrine to human genius and creativity. It was to this room that he would retire when he needed to think and contemplate in absolute silence. He seldom invited anyone else to join him. I had been in his employ for more than a year, in fact, before I even learned that the room existed.

One evening following dinner, Lodge unexpectedly became interested in transforming my lack of education in art appreciation. He insisted that I join him in the *atelier* for a lesson.

The lights came on automatically as we entered the room. As we stood in front of a painting, the lighting of the other canvases dimmed, allowing the one we were contemplating to stand out clearly. It did not matter, however; the Fragonards seemed to supply their own light.

"I didn't know much about Fragonard before I acquired this house," Lodge told me. "He is not that well known in the United States. That is a shame, because he did exquisite things with his paint brushes and palette. He attacked his canvases with fire and inspiration. They often seem to deal with trivial subjects, but one of his paintings usually reveals more of the inner nature of spirit than one hundred canvases by a lesser artist.

"Look at this one, for example," he enthused, gesturing toward a canvas called *The Private Park*. It was a small canvas painted in one of the formal gardens popular in his day. A group of children played among the statuary in front of a bridge in the gardens, while their mothers chatted among themselves. "Is it just the idea that these people are gathered in a private nook of the garden—or is it a painting about privacy? Do any of us have privacy? What does privacy conceal? Why are we so protective of it? Look in the shadows—Fragonard used the dark tones almost as skillfully, I think, as Rembrandt. What secrets do the vines and shrubs conceal—the secrets of centuries, perhaps? The women have their secrets; their husbands have theirs; their lovers have others. The children will grow up and have secrets all of their own.

"We all go to elaborate pains to protect our secrets and preserve our privacy. Why? Why spend so much time guarding our secrets, when we could be putting our talents and joy to work, inspiring others, helping others, and uplifting them?"

He turned to me, as if he had previously been talking to the canvas. "Do you have secrets you try to hide, Morgan?"

I was taken aback by the abruptness of the question, but I tried to answer it honestly. "There are certainly things I have done that I am not proud of, but I don't think I try to conceal them. I don't think anything I have done would ruin me if it became known."

"The best secrets are those that can be shared with all—the secrets of the ages, the secrets of life," Lodge said by way of reply. "Fragonard peered into the secret lives of those women, and revealed them in this painting, don't you think? This is not a painting that hides secrets; it reveals them. It announces them, as though they were marriage banns, to be read in public. It declares the secrets of the heart and soul in lovely shades of boisterous color. It affirms the basic decency of these people."

He gave me a few moments to let that idea sink in, then added: "The need for privacy or secrecy is the breeding ground of crime. We do something we do not want others to know about. So we begin to hide and cover up. We invent lies. We tell stories. We compound the problem. We may even decide to kill.

"That's why we need civilization," he pronounced, looking at me with triumphant satisfaction, as though he just solved the last remaining mystery of life.

"Civilization tames the criminal breast. I almost wish we didn't have to lock up criminals in penitentiaries. An art museum would be a much better place to confine them, so that their brutish nature could be refined." He laughed, almost to himself. "Of course, the sentence would have to be for thirty or forty lifetimes, in order for the treatment to work!"

I admitted that the artwork hanging in his home had a way of lifting me up above dark thoughts of crime—but added that if he made me stare at *The Scream* for very long, I would probably be moved to murder *him.*

"Well stated, Morgan! You have the soul of an artist within you after all! Who would have believed it possible?"

I decided that one insight was my limit for the evening. But Lodge was just hitting his stride.

"So tell me, Morgan, which do you think is true? Does art imitate life or does life imitate art?" We were standing in front of a larger canvas entitled *The Nervous Model.* A young girl had been hired by a painter to act as a model. She had come to work accompanied by a chaperon, probably her mother. She did not know what to expect. Would the artist ask her to model in the nude? Would he make amorous advances? What was his purpose?

Lodge chuckled. "Fragó must have faced this situation a thousand times in his life. You might call this painting "Innocence Meeting Experience." Innocence needs Experience in order to grow. But Innocence is afraid of losing something important—its purity or its naïveté—in the process.

"This is one of the purposes of great art—to strip away the clothes in which we hide our inhibitions and our lack of experience. We cannot know truth unless we see it unclothed, unadorned. Every insight into life must be seen as a bare essence before it makes sense to us."

The third canvas we examined was a nude bathing herself in a secluded forest stream. It took away my breath for a moment; the particular pose strongly suggested that the bather was doing more than just taking a swim. There was no title to the piece, but Lodge said it reminded him of the Greek myth of the goddess Diana bathing. In the myth, Diana is accidentally seen by Actæon, a Greek prince. She punishes him for his transgression by transforming him into a stag. His friends then hunt him down and kill him, not knowing it is actually the prince.

"Sometimes we learn things about life we are not meant to learn," Lodge mused. "When we behold a piece of art, we are something like Actæon secretly beholding a goddess. We are given an opportunity to glimpse the divine. We just want to make sure that we are not discovered—and not transformed into venison."

"Are you suggesting," I asked, "that this

painting of an unclothed girl cavorting in the stream has any meaning besides an appeal to the lascivious? I would imagine a lot of inmates would like to have this painting pinned up in their cells—and they wouldn't be refined a whole lot by it, either."

"Ah, Morgan, your puritanical background betrays you!" Lodge exclaimed. "This is not just a picture of a naked girl—it is a testimony to the need for each of us to find refreshment daily in the joy and beauty of spirit."

"I don't know," I replied, puzzled. "It seems almost lewd to me. Look at how—"

"—the water courses through her thighs." Lodge finished my observation for me. "That's the focus of the whole piece. It reminds us of our need to approach the fountainheads of life with joy instead of inhibition. This is one reason why artists usually end up living slightly Bohemian lives. They shatter society's narrow moral conventions and prudery. Fragonard was a master at it. He was attuned to the joys and delights of life—and the role of sexuality in it all."

A sharp ring several rooms away interrupted his reveries. It was the doorbell. I went to see who it was. It was the mayor.

"Good evening, Jack," I said as I opened the door. "What brings you by at this hour?"

"A murder of some consequence, I am afraid," Jack replied. "Is Lodge about?"

Lodge appeared as the mayor made his inquiry. "At your service as always, Jack," he said. "How can we help you this evening?"

"A local artist—his name was Robert Hubert, I believe—was found murdered a short while ago. It appears that he was strangled with a man's belt while cleaning up his brushes after painting all day."

"Robert Hubert, you say?" Lodge mused. "I think I have heard of him. He had a promising career ahead of him."

"Well, it is a promise that won't be kept," said the mayor. "He is quite dead."

"Was there a struggle?" I asked.

"So far, the evidence suggests that he was surprised from behind and throttled without being able to defend himself. But we are handling it as a crime of passion—the bruises on the throat indicate that he was strangled with great violence, almost defiance. Nothing was taken from the studio."

"Who is the woman?" Lodge interrupted. "I presume she was the artist's model."

The mayor looked at Lodge long and hard. Even though he was well acquainted with Lodge's intuitive abilities, their demonstration always brought a moment of incredulity.

"He spent the last hour with Fragonard," I inserted, trying to be flippant. "He has nude models on the brain."

Jack recovered in a moment. "The woman involved—we have been calling her the woman in blue, after the half-finished painting sitting on Hubert's easel—is a model in her late twenties named Margaret Gerard. She is not a suspect.

"The body was discovered by another artist, who had the studio next to Hubert's. He was in the habit of looking in on Hubert each evening, exchanging a little artistic small talk, and then saying good-bye as he left. Tonight, there was nothing to say. Hubert was already dead.

"The artist-next-door called the police, to notify them of the homicide. When the first officers arrived, they observed the painting of the woman in blue on the easel. Rummaging through Hubert's records, they found the name 'Maraget Gerard' and her phone number. They called her and asked her to return to the studio. When she returned and spied the artist sprawled on the floor, dead, she broke into hysterical crying and continued for at least twenty minutes."

"Why did you rule her out as a suspect?" Lodge inquired.

"Her reaction to seeing the artist dead was so strong and genuine it could not have been staged," Jack replied.

"Quite so," Lodge confirmed. "Is the woman in blue still at the studio?"

"Yes," the mayor replied. "And so is the body. I ordered the detective to leave everything in place until you could arrive."

"Good," Lodge replied. "Of course, I do not actually have to visit the crime scene, but in this case it may prove helpful."

We climbed into the mayor's waiting limousine and were driven to the studio, which was located downtown in an old brewery district. An abandoned warehouse had been converted into studios for artists, sculptors, and musicians. Today it was surrounded by police cars and ambulances and cordoned off with yellow tape. The other tenants who had not yet gone home were growing more hostile by the moment, as the police would not let any of them leave. As the head detective put it, they were all suspects.

Seeing the angry artists, Lodge told Jack he might as well let them go home.

"None of them killed Hubert," he said. "You are just making a group of voters angry by detaining them here."

Reaching the studio, Lodge listened impatiently while the head detective filled him in on what they had discovered so far, which was little more than the fact that an artist who was alive a few hours before, when the model had left for the day, was now quite dead, and he did not choose to leave this life voluntarily. After a minute or so, Lodge silenced the detective with a wave of his hand. He had heard enough.

"I must ask the model one question," Lodge began. Margaret—the woman in blue—looked up abruptly, with confusion in her eyes. "No," Lodge comforted her, "you are not under suspicion. But even though you had already left before the foul deed occurred, I believe something you did—or did not—somehow precipitated this crime."

Margaret turned to the head detective. "Don't worry, ma'am—" he said soothingly. "I didn't understand what he said, either. Just answer his questions."

"My question is this," Lodge continued. "Were your clothes as disshevelled when you left the studio as they are now? Or is their disarray entirely due to the fact that you have been shocked and grieving since you came back?"

"I-I do not know," the model replied. "I am a model. I have worked for Robert for years. I seldom wear my street clothes to pose. I change into something else. But this time he wanted to paint me as I am, in my own clothing. So I did not change before leaving tonight. You can look at the easel to see that I am telling the truth. That is the way he was painting me."

I went over to the easel and studied the portrait in progress briefly. It was an oil of a woman dressed in blue—the very woman who was sitting, sobbing, before us, and dressed in the same clothes, although not dishevelled. It was eerie, to say the least. Although fully clothed, her face bore the same expression of ecstasy I had observed on the face of the secret bather painted by Fragonard. I blinked and shook my head, thinking I was transposing one image onto another. I was not. Either the model or the artist—or both—had been attuned to the same enthrallment as Lodge and I had been talking about earlier in the evening.

"She's right," I hollered to Lodge.

"I ran back to the studio after the police called. That was probably when my blouse became untucked."

"Quite so," said Lodge, "and yet that does not explain everything that happened today, does it?"

"What do you mean?" asked the woman in blue.

"What I mean," Lodge replied, "cannot be phrased delicately. Earlier today, not once but twice, you removed your clothes not to model in the nude, but to make love to the dead man."

The woman in blue blushed to a complementary color. "Sir! I have never made love to a dead man!" she said indignantly.

"Of course not," Lodge said soothingly. "He was not yet dead. But you did make love to the artist before he died, did you not?"

"How could you possibly know that!"

"Madam," said Lodge distinctly, "I am a thought detective. I solve crimes by reading people's emotions and thoughts. You have been sitting here blubbering ever since I arrived, grieving not over the loss of a friend or employer, but over the death of a lover. Every sob you have uttered has spoken volumes."

The woman backed up in her chair, as though she wanted to put as much space between herself and this new devil as she could.

"That's not fair," she spluttered. "This was a private matter. You have no right—"

"I agree. But a man has been murdered—a man you loved. Certainly you want to discover his murderer as much as we do?"

The woman in blue whispered. "Yes."

"Good. Then answer a second question. Who is John Rousseau?"

The model lost all of her color. "John Rousseau? I haven't thought of John Rousseau in a year. How do you know about him? And what on earth does he have to do with the death of Robert?"

"John Rousseau is the man who strangled the dead man lying behind the easel," Lodge announced.

"How can you know this?" the woman in blue shrieked, almost hysterical.

"It's all in the mind," Lodge explained.

Everyone pretended not to hear him. "Do you know this John Rousseau?" asked the head detective.

"Of course not," Lodge replied. "I would not be able to pick him out of a police line up. But the woman in blue knows him. She had a long running affair with him. It is true that she dumped him more than a year ago, but he has continued to carry the torch for her, as they say in cheap detective novels.

"Whenever we have sex with another person, we create a strong psychological bond that becomes a permanent part of our character. This bond is telepathic as well as sexual. This is the reason why it can be dangerous to have sex outside of marriage, because these very strong ties remain, and any pairing of lovers will continue to commune with each other at deep emotional levels, for as long as they both shall live. It cannot be stopped—at least not by the average person. In cases where people have been highly promiscuous, they end up with an emotional overload, and this tends to make any kind of commitment or sharing next to impossible. Such people actually lose a vital element of their humanity.

"Even though you thought you had ended your fling with John a year ago," Lodge continued, addressing the model, "you were still emotionally and sexually tied to him at an unconscious level of character. What you did not know was that John had a low level ability to communicate telepathically. In fact, he has dabbled in sex magic and takes his sexual conquests—including you—quite seriously. So, when your relationship with Robert ceased being platonic and artistic, and became sexual and passionate, John became quite agitated. The gratification he had previously experienced through his relationship with you reversed itself and became a sense of emptiness. He began to choke on his own unrequited desires and passions, which backed up in his awareness like a clogged sewer. At the same time, he was consumed with an irrational jealousy. He was responding viscerally to the pleasure you were giving Robert—and receiving in return. At first, John thought he was developing some kind of nervous condition. But then he awoke one morning with a vivid dream—a very vivid dream of you having intercourse with another man. Then he knew. He did not know who the man was—but he had figured out who the woman was: *you*. He tracked you down and shadowed you for a few days. He was watching you the whole day today, and saw you have sex with Robert. He waited until you left, entered the studio while Robert was cleaning up, and strangled him with his belt."

Lodge turned to the police. "I expect he is trying to leave the city even as we speak. I would recommend closing down all possible exits until you apprehend him."

It was then that I spoke up. "How on earth did you discern all of that, Lodge? Did he leave a psychic spoor, or what?"

"There would be a psychic trail, yes, but I did not need to try to discern that," said Lodge, laughing. "There is no human drive that leaves a stronger residue than sexuality. I just read the portions of Margaret's subconscious that had telepathed the message to John in the first place. It is not especially pleasant to be exposed to so much steam and raw heat, but the link to John was easy to follow.

"Of course, I did not conclude that John was the murderer based on Margaret's passions. It never occurred to her that John even cared about her any more, certainly not to the point of committing murder. But the moment her passion tied me into John, the whole picture became clear. He had seen a secret he was not meant to see, and had turned himself into a beast—a beast that we are now trying to hunt down and capture."

"John is not the victim of a woman scorned, let alone a goddess. He is a victim of his own feeble efforts at sex magic backfiring and trapping him in the very snares he so often tried to set for women.

"That is always the end of anyone, male or female, who tries to ensnare others with sex magic. The only one who is trapped is the person who tries to manipulate others for his or her own depraved pleasure.

"Let this be a lesson, Morgan. Great art reveals the ideals of life. It can never be indecent or lewd. But human passion is another thing entirely. Within it, you can find the entire spectrum of pettiness and degradation.

"This crime tells us the story of humanity. Tonight, brutishness murdered artistry. But do not worry. Tomorrow, art will gain the upper hand, and cleanse man's brutish habits."

Five

The Brush Off

The mayor had not cracked a smile for weeks, even though he had much to celebrate. The city had launched a new program to reduce crime and drugs, and it was working beyond everyone's expectations. Test scores in the local public schools had reached all-time highs. Unemployment throughout the city had plunged to an all-time low. But Jack was unable to enjoy any of these triumphs; he, too, had hit an all-time low.

Through no fault of his own, Jack was being hammered unrelentingly by the press. A murder had occurred, and no arrests had been made, although two months had passed. Even worse, it looked as if Jack was shielding a colleague of his—a member of the city council.

Here are the facts the mayor presented to us when he first called on Lodge with a plea for assistance. A young woman—her name was Jill Hatch—had been murdered. A cufflink belonging to Councilman Dan Merton was found near the body. Its mate was found in Dan's jewelry box. Investigators also found semen on Miss Hatch's body and clothes. DNA tests were run, and produced a perfect match with the DNA of Dan Merton. Adam Goodman, the police chief, wanted to arrest Dan immediately, but the mayor prevented him. Dan, it seems, had the perfect alibi—three poker pals who swore he had spent the whole evening playing five-card stud with him the night the foul deed was done. The wife of the poker pal who had hosted the game supported the alibi even further, confirming that Dan had been sitting at the card table in their rec room, drinking Dos XX's beer.

In addition, Dan flatly denied ever knowing the victim—and there was no evidence to suggest that he had—or that he had a motive to kill her. Corinna Caxton, our district attorney, flatly dismissed these claims, however, theorizing that Dan had picked up the victim in a bar, went to her apartment for sex, and had gotten out of control. The only problem with this line of reasoning was that Miss Hatch was not known as "that type of girl."

The mayor sat across from Lodge. "I tell you, Walter," Jack said, "I don't know how much longer I can withstand the pressure. The press is howling for Dan's head—they want me to arrest him and try him for first degree murder. They think the alibis are phony."

"Of course," Lodge agreed. "Rash action is always preferred by the press to right action."

"It looks bad for Dan," the mayor added. "I have never liked the man, but in my heart I think he is innocent."

"Your instincts are as sharp as ever, your Honor," Lodge replied. "Dan is guilty of all kinds of indiscretions, but not murder."

"You've solved the case?" the mayor asked, incredulously. "Already?"

"I haven't actually solved the case," Lodge replied, "but I do know that Dan is innocent—at least of murder. Now, if you want to talk about taking an occasional bribe, or being in bed with the unions, or cheating on his wife, that is another story. But not murder. Still, I can't help thinking..."

Lodge abruptly left the room—mentally—launching himself into another dimension. I had learned from long experience that he was examining various possibilities, perhaps hunting through "the Archives"—unconscious levels of mind—for invisible leads. He would rejoin us whenever he chose to return.

In the meanwhile, I entertained Jack with small talk. I regaled him with stories of my days in the military police, hoping to distract him from the pressures he was facing. In return, he entertained me with selected anecdotes from his mayoral campaign. But I could tell his heart was not fully into story-telling. He was truly distressed that a sordid scandal could distract so much from the serious business of running a city.

An hour later, Lodge came back to us. He addressed Jack first.
"Go ahead and arrest Dan," he advised.
"On what charges?" the mayor asked.
"Why, on first degree murder, of course," Lodge replied crisply.
"But you said just an hour ago that he is innocent."
"Of murdering this woman, yes." replied Lodge. "But not of slaughtering his public trust. Give me a little leeway here, Jack."
He turned to me. "Morgan, I want you to make some checks."
He directed me to come up with a list of every woman that had worked for Dan and left his employment in the last five years, and provide short biographical sketches of each. With that, Jack headed back to city hall—and I plunged into my assignment.
The research was easy enough. I used my computer to hook into the employment files at city hall—with Jack's full cooperation and knowledge, of course. Those military stories

paid off, after all. I connected to city hall through the internet, and downloaded files on everyone who had worked for Dan in the last five years. It took about thirty minutes before I was able to present Lodge with the requested information.

"No," said Lodge when he had finished scanning my report.

"No?" I echoed.

"This list does not include the woman I am looking for. Perhaps she worked on one of his campaigns, and then was not hired for a job in his office. Ah-ha! That must be it! A case of unrequited patronage." He sent me back to my computer, to come up with a list of people who had worked for Dan in his last two campaigns. Unfortunately, my computer could not provide me with that information, so I had to resort to superior means. I broke into Dan's office and examined his files. Well, it was hardly breaking and entering, since the mayor gave me the key. But I did not have Dan's permission. I "borrowed" the files that I felt were relevant to our investigation.

This time Lodge's eyes lit up.

"Sally Desmond. That's the one. I need a lock of her hair."

I gave him an odd look.

"So we can test her DNA," he added.

"She's the murderer?" I asked.

"So far, she has only killed one person—Jill Hatch. But Jill was not her real target. It is Dan she wants to 'brush off.' She wants to see him executed for the crime she actually committed."

"Why?" I asked.

"She became very upset with Dan when he failed to offer her a job once he was elected. She was sure she would get one—after all, she had been giving him all the sex he wanted throughout the whole campaign. She became quite angry, and actually accused Dan to his face of using her. Which is hilarious in a way, because it is clear that she was trying to use Dan. But the perpetrator seldom sees himself—or herself—as nasty or scheming. He much prefers to see himself as the ultimate victim.

"Anyway, I need a lock of her hair. You can get it for me, can't you?"

I thought we were beginning to walk the tightrope a bit too close to the edge, but Lodge dismissed my protests with a wave of his hand.

"She thinks she has committed the perfect crime," Lodge said. "She deliberately killed Jill Hatch in cold blood because she did not know her. She thinks she cannot be linked to this death in any way. So she is not expecting company. Besides, she is out of town for the weekend. You'll be fine."

So I broke into the home of Sally Desmond. I headed straight for her bedroom, where I found her dressing table. It was loaded with all kinds of ointments, creams, waters, powders, and rouges—a shrine to Vanity very much like millions of other dressing tables across the land. It was easy enough to extract some locks from her hair brush. I also managed to retrieve a small, lidless jar carelessly thrown in the back of one of her dressing table drawers. I absent-mindedly wondered what it had held; there was now a dried-up layer of some substance still clinging to the mouth of the jar. I was about to put it back where I found it, when I noticed a faint smell of crabapple filling the room. I put the jar in a plastic bag and slipped it into my pocket instead.

I returned from my treasure hunt and presented my booty to Lodge.

"Now what?" I asked.

"We send these items off to a crime lab for DNA testing. And then we wait."

"For what?"

"For the results. And for Dan's trial, of course."

"You are going to let an innocent man go to trial?" I asked.

"Everyone is presumed innocent going *into* a trial," Lodge laughed, delighted in hoisting me on my own petard. "That's why we have trials—to discover, perhaps even rationally, who is innocent and who is not. It doesn't always work that way, but it is better than most other systems mankind has devised. Like drowning supposed witches in the river.

"Besides, Dan is only innocent of murder, and there is no evidence to convict him of anything else. The trial should be enough to embarrass him into resigning. Then justice will have been done—twice."

The trial did not start well for Dan. The prosecution, headed by Corinna Caxton herself, dredged up every bit of slime Dan had ever stepped in, wrung it out in open court, and left his reputation in ruins. What the prosecution was not allowed to present in court the press eagerly exposed in subsequent editions. I was beginning to suspect that there was a gaping leak leading directly from the prosecutor's office to the city desk.

Corinna pursued her prey without mercy. *She* was not presuming the defendant to be innocent. "Just an ardent feminist applying justice as she sees fit," quipped Lodge. "Quite a show, isn't it? If only Phineas could be here."

"Phineas?" I inquired.

"P.T. Barnum," clarified Lodge. "He always loved good theater."

I was even beginning to feel sorry for Dan, but Lodge dispelled that notion. "He is a rat. He deserves every bit of the humiliation that has come up so far—and a lot more. I just wish the court could go into some of the things he has done in past lives. He has earned every ounce of shame and scorn they are heaping upon him. He is not an innocent bystander."

Lodge stopped for a minute, fixated his eyes two feet in front of him, and then scowled. "And the rat has not yet resigned. I am beginning to think he has no conscience at all. The man is a pathological scoundrel."

I had seldom heard Lodge speak so intensely about anyone else, even a criminal. To hear him describe a public servant in such terms made the impact of his words even greater.

The one bright spot for the defense during Corinna's presentation of the city's case came in its cross examination of the coroner. The witness had just finished testifying about the semen he had found on the victim's body and clothes—semen that matched Dan Merton's DNA.

"Did you examine the body for sexual contact?" the defense attorney asked.

"Of course," the coroner replied. "I just described the semen I found."

"That is not what I asked," the defense attorney replied, a bit curtly. "I asked if there was any evidence of sexual intercourse—other than the semen you so graphically placed on the victim's person. Were there abrasions or swellings, for example? Was there any sign of penetration?"

The witness fidgeted a bit. "Now that you mention it, no. I just assumed that the presence of the semen indicated that sex had been involved."

"Perhaps it was," the defense attorney suggested. "But would it also be consistent with the facts to theorize that whoever killed Jill Hatch just poured Dan Merton's semen on the victim's body and clothes and smeared it around?"

Predictably, Miss Caxton objected, claiming the attorney was leading the witness.

The defense attorney protested that he was only trying to establish an alternate possibility—a possibility that had not been addressed by the prosecution. The judge agreed. But it was only a minor dent in the heavy armor of the state's case—a mere flicker of doubt.

Finally, Miss Caxton rested, and the defense was directed to present its case. It called the three witnesses that swore Dan was with them playing poker. But under cross examination, the prosecution managed to paint each one of his buddies as an unreliable witness. All of them, it turned out, had been involved in embarrassing ways in one or more of Dan's escapades. Each had a powerful motive to protect their friend by lying about the poker game.

The defense did score some points when they called the wife of the party's host. Dos XX's is not a common alcoholic beverage in this country, and the wife produced a receipt proving that she had bought a six-pack of Dos XX's the morning before the poker game—"just for Dan"—as she said brightly. The prosecution let that bit of evidence go unchallenged, confident that it was not enough of an alibi to get Dan off the hook.

Then the defense started its counter punch. It called a crime lab technician who had analyzed certain bits of evidence submitted anonymously to him by "a friend of the court."

The prosecution protested again, demanding to know why the defense had not shared this evidence with them. "It is your job to prove the guilt of my client," the attorney replied, "not my job to prevent you from looking stupid. I actually do not know how the evidence was obtained. But I shall use it to prove that Dan Merton did not kill Jill Hatch."

The judge admitted that he was eager to see how this could be done.

The attorney resumed questioning the lab technician. "What is the first item you were asked to examine?"

"A piece of hair," he replied.

"What kind of hair?" the attorney continued.

"Human hair. Female. Blond."

"And did you run DNA tests on the hair?"

"Yes. I tried to match it to everyone involved in the case," the technician continued, "but the only match was to hair found at the crime scene but not linked to any known person."

"Do you know where the hair came from?" the attorney asked.

"No," the technician replied, "although I presume that at some point in time it was attached to a lady's head."

There was a moment of tittering in the court room. The lawyer continued.

"Please identify the second item."

"It's an ordinary plastic cosmetics bottle, a kind that can be bought in any drug store. Women use them to transfer hand cream or other cosmetics to smaller bottles—you know, when they travel."

"Was hand cream the content of this bottle?"

"No."

"What was the bottle's contents?"

"Human semen. From a male."

This time the attorney laughed. "I had presumed that," he said. "And did you run DNA tests on the semen?"

"Yes."

"What did you find?"

"The semen in the bottle exactly matches the sample of semen supplied to the court by Dan Merton."

"Did the bottle of semen provide any other clues?" asked the attorney.

"Yes. There were fingerprints on the bottle. But again, they did not match any of the fingerprints gathered by the police in this case."

"They did not match the fingerprints of Dan Merton?"

"No, sir."

"Did they match any other fingerprints?" the attorney inquired.

"Yes. The anonymous source included records of both the DNA and fingerprints taken of a woman, a Miss Sally Desmond. Both the DNA of the hair strand I analyzed and the fingerprints on the small jar matched the samples exactly."

There was a general ooh and aah in the court room, but no one knew exactly why, because none of the evidence yet made any sense. The attorney excused the crime lab techician, then made an unprecedented request.

"I would like to call the anonymous source of these items, if he or she is in the courtroom."

None other than Walter Lodge rose solemnly and strode to the witness chair. "I am the no-longer anonymous source of that information."

"Would you please identify yourself?"

"Walter J. Lodge, Thought Detective."

"What does a thought detective do?"

"He examines the evidence of a case logically, to see if it holds together."

"Don't the police do that?"

"They should—but they seldom do. They let their professional pride and desire to solve cases inhibit clear thinking."

A murmur rippled through the courtroom.

"What is your interest in this case?"

"I am a friend of the mayor. He asked me to investigate the known facts in this case, because he believed Dan had not killed Jill Hatch."

"And how did you come by these items?"

"They were found in the possession of Miss Sally Desmond."

"And what do they mean?"

"They mean that Dan Merton, for all of his

other sins against this community, did not kill Jill Hatch. He did not even know her. Jill Hatch was murdered by Sally Desmond."

I glanced over at the crime reporter for the local newspaper in time to see him realize, for a brief moment in time, that he had led a lynching party against an innocent man. Then his arrogance returned, and he resumed his usual air of journalistic irresponsibility.

"Why?" the defense attorney asked of Lodge.

"To frame Dan. She had had an affair with Dan while working for his campaign. She expected to be given a patronage job in the government when Dan was elected. But Dan brushed her off and would have nothing more to do with her. She got mad—and decided to get even. So she arranged a "chance meeting" with Dan one evening, and coaxed him into having sex with her again—at her home. It was not a difficult sale to close, as you might imagine. She made sure that the results were, uh, messy enough that she could collect some of his semen, once he had left. She preserved it in a small plastic jar until she had a chance to murder Miss Hatch a few days later. She then carefully spread Dan's semen on the dead woman's body and clothes.

"I want to emphasize that Miss Desmond

had no reason to kill Miss Hatch—which is precisely why she did. She deliberately picked a victim that could not be linked to her in any way. This is the reason why she is not in the court room today—but Dan is.

"Miss Desmond had also been thoughtful enough to steal one of Dan's cufflinks and place it at the crime scene, to make it all the easier for the police to incriminate Dan. It was an admirable scheme—except for one detail."

"And what was that?"

"Miss Desmond had no idea how obvious bitterness can be. It advertises itself and leaves a trail that even a blind man could follow. When the mayor asked me to help him solve the murder of Jill Hatch, I immediately became aware of a powerful presence of bitterness. I just followed the trail of Miss Desmond's bitterness in my mind—and it led me straight to her."

The judge could not help himself. "Fascinating!" he exclaimed.

The jury, being more superstitious in nature, looked at one another quizzically—hoping they would not have to pass judgment on this latest testimony. The judge obliged, declaring Dan "innocent of the charges."

Lodge then turned to Corinna. "When you go to arrest Miss Desmond this afternoon, you might want to inquire as to her motive. She may just tell you the truth. She was hoping to let the jury murder Dan for her—she framed him for a murder he did not commit, so that he would be executed by the state. Judging from the way the trial was going, I would guess that she almost succeeded."

Six

The Night Nothing Happened

Lodge never took precautions for his personal safety. He refused to carry a gun or weapon of any kind. He employed no bodyguards—he hired me to "do his dirty work," as he put it, not to protect him. He kept a low profile if at all possible, but if required, he would walk openly and fearlessly into a crowd of thugs without a thought for his safety. "I am armed with my mind," he would say whenever I questioned this lack of suitable defenses. "Why should I rely on inferior mechanisms?"

And so, it was a surprise one crisp autumn evening when Lodge suggested that I arrange for suitable protection for the house. "There are going to be some strange doings tonight," he remarked cryptically. "I want to be prepared."

The great Lodge afraid for his life? I could hardly believe that any adventure could be so perilous. But instead of doubting the content of Lodge's instructions, I merely asked for an elaboration. I had already learned the futility of questioning any decision Lodge made.

"How much protection do you think we will need?" I asked.

"Oh, one man should be enough," Lodge replied. "Two would be a waste of money, just to keep each other company."

I made the arrangements, calling on the services of a good friend of mine, Henry Saxon, a police sergeant who happened to be off duty. I had known Henry since he served with me in the military police; in fact, I had been the one who had helped him secure his present position in the constabulary. He and his wife had recently lost their only son after a desperate battle with pneumonia, and neither one of them had taken the loss well. But Henry at least had his work to distract him. His wife still had two young daughters at home, but refused to find solace in raising them. All she could focus on was her loss.

Henry was pleased by the prospect of making some extra money—and, of course, delighted to be involved in our caper, whatever it might be. He could already envision himself, years later, telling his grandchildren about the night he spent protecting Walter J. Lodge. It's the sort of stuff that inspires legends.

Henry arrived and took up a post on the porch. Lodge had suggested that he might as well enjoy the warmth and lighting of the kitchen, but Henry would hear none of it. How could he protect Lodge from the kitchen? Only the porch would do. Lodge acquiesced without protest, retiring to the great parlor, as he called it, to pick up his well-worn copy of *Leaves of Grass*.

"Are we starting a new case?" I inquired, trying mightily to camouflage my desire to learn what adventure was brewing.

Lodge replied monsyllabically. "No."

"Are you expecting a visitor?" I pursued. "The mayor perhaps?"

"No," replied Lodge again. He set down his volume of Whitman. "While asking intelligent questions is a noble art, and highly commendable, using this art to launch a hunting expedition into another person's mind is a sign of disrespect. It is also dangerous—it almost always leads to runaway cases of leaping to unfounded conclusions."

"Well," I stammered, "You have raised my expectations."

"No, I have not," Lodge objected. "I simply asked you to hire a man for the night. You have taken that request and fantasized some Byzantine Miss Marple plot from it. Careful thinkers never let that happen. They examine facts, not speculations. They live in reality, not fantasy. And they never, ever leap to conclusions. The potential for falling on their faces is too great."

With that, Lodge went back to his poetry. I crossed over to the far wall, which was lined with bookcases, found a collection of short stories to plunge into, and went back to my chair. But I couldn't get into the tales; I was just too absorbed with my speculations. What was going to happen? Should I fetch my gun?

At 11 p.m., we took Henry some hot chocolate and sweets.

"Begging your pardon, sir," he asked Lodge. "but it seems awfully quiet out tonight. Just what are we looking for?"

"Quiet is precisely what we are looking for," replied Lodge. "And hoping for and praying for. I have found that if you go out looking specifically for mischief, all kinds of mischief are apt to find you. No, it is far, far safer to go out looking for peace and joyfulness. Expect quietness, and you may actually find it. Create quietness, and it shall be yours."

"But it is hard to stay alert to danger when all is quiet, sir," Henry replied.

"That is because you have only experienced the rush of adrenalin in the face of danger. You need to teach yourself to be thrilled by the onrush of a new idea, a new understanding—to be excited by the prospect of unexpected beauty or an act of kindness, let alone an evening when absolutely nothing happens.

"I, myself, have been meditating on the value of silence tonight. There is so much that people could know, if they just practiced silence occasionally. But they block it out, preferring the noise of talkative people or blaring music to the inner whispers of silence."

With that, Lodge announced he was going to retire. Normally, I would have gone to my own quarters in the updated carriage house, but I could not bear to miss out on whatever excitement was still brewing. So I announced that I would sleep on the sofa, a big, bulky piece of stuffed furniture that would be almost as comfortable as my own bed. Lodge smiled thinly, shaking his head.

"As you wish," he said, and went upstairs. "Sleep well."

As it turned out, I was the only one who did not sleep well. In the silence of the early morning, I could tell from the muffled cadence of rhythmic breathing issuing from upstairs that Lodge was stirred by no anxiety. At the same time, the boisterous snoring coming from the porch amply demonstrated that moonlighting takes its toll on even the most seasoned officer.

On the couch, meanwhile, I was fretting and

stewing. Why was nothing happening? This was supposed to be a night of great adventure. Instead, it was rapidly turning into a night of sleep deprivation—at least for me.

About 3 a.m., I thought I heard a gun fire. "This is it," I muttered, leaping to my feet. But as I peered out the front window, I saw that it was only a car backfiring, as a neighbor returned from another hard night of carousing. Out on the porch, Henry had not even awakened.

Twenty minutes later, as I was just about to drift into a light sleep, I heard a cat challenging a fellow male who had dared trespass on his territory. But after several minutes of strident hissing and a few choice feline oaths, they went their separate ways. The darkness fell silent again. Finally, I drifted off to sleep.

I awoke about 7 a.m. to behold a fully dressed Lodge standing in front of me, talking to Henry.

"You had better go now," Lodge was telling Henry. He handed him a check for his night's services. "I just got a call from your chief. Your wife has been taken to the hospital. She is not in good shape. You had better go see her there."

"The hospital?" gasped Henry. "What happened?"

"She had a bit of a breakdown, I'm afraid," said Lodge. "She started smashing dishes and windows a couple of hours ago. It woke your daughters, and the eldest called the chief. He dispatched a couple of officers. They subdued her and took her to the hospital. Your kids are there, too."

Henry grabbed his hat and ran to his car.

I was left staring at Lodge in utter disbelief.

"What was that all about?" I asked. "First you have me hire Henry to protect you on a night when absolutely nothing happened, and now it turns out that he should have been at home instead. Sometimes, I just do not understand you."

Lodge smiled. "You never understand me, Morgan, but sometimes you misunderstand me less than other times. Tonight, you have outdone yourself.

"The facts of the case are these. Henry's wife just went on a murderous rampage, breaking out windows with her bare hands, slashing perfectly good furniture, and pushing over a china cabinet. Had Henry been sleeping at home, he would probably be dead by now. As it was, his wife merely managed to cut herself up pretty bad and damage the house.

"Even though I did not know Henry before

last evening, I became aware of his danger through his connection with you, the moment you walked into the dining room for dinner. I surmised that the simplest way to handle the situation was to ask you to provide a bodyguard, which you did. I knew you would think of Henry first, which you did.

"In fact, you played your part in this little drama exceedingly well, except for your curious insistence on inventing fantastic scenarios and jumping to conclusions that were in no way warranted. When are you going to learn that jumping to conclusions is a good way to end up in the wrong place?

"In your case, you ended up with a night of no sleep. And, rather than learn something from it, you compound the problem by scolding me for saving Henry's life!"

I tried to stammer out an apology.

Lodge laughed again. "No need for that, my good friend. When will you learn that it's all in the mind? Now, go help Henry at the hospital."

Seven

Thanksgiving

It was not like Lodge to be anything but straightforward. And so, I was surprised, as Thanksgiving approached one year, when Lodge began dropping regular hints that he might like to be invited to join me at my family gathering that year. My folks lived about two hours away, and I always joined them for the major holidays, unless our business kept me from making it. My sisters also usually attended. I had often asked Lodge if he would like to come to these holiday gatherings, but he had always declined, generally on some silly premise such as "Thanksgiving is not a fair deal for the turkeys. Now a goose—they are as silly as we say they are. I would have no compunction consuming a goose. But I stand with Benjamin Franklin: the turkey is a noble, all-American bird." I suspected that it was just a polite way of saying he preferred his own company.

But this year was turning out to be different, with Lodge initiating the change.

"Will you be joining your family this year

for Thanksgiving, Morgan?" he asked me, about a week before the affair. I confirmed that I was.

A few days later, he stopped me in the gallery hall, so called because of the magnificent twin landscapes by Thomas Cole that hung in radiant glory at each end of the hall, with works by lesser artists adorning the walls in between. "What kind of entertainment does your family indulge in on these occasions? I hope they are not one of those groups that hypnotize themselves by sitting in front of their television sets watching football all day long!" I assured him that they were not—although I was not quite sure that gossipping about other family members all day long would actually be deemed a respectable alternative.

Two days later, he was back at it. "Are your sisters coming in from out of town to join the family?" My sisters—Fay is married and May is not—both pursue careers in cities several hours away from the family home. I must have looked surprised by the query, because he hastened to add, "Of course, I know they are. But it seemed rude to assume so without asking first." He sighed, as though the burden of social niceties was almost too much to bear. "Now it seems rude to be sticking my nose into your family matters."

I decided I had tortured Lodge long enough in pretending to ignore his many hints. I let the poor guy off the hook. "Would you care to join us for Thanksgiving, Lodge?"

He feigned indifference. "Huh? Oh, you know I never go in for that sort of thing. I would be totally out of place—it's your family, after all, not mine. You would want to tell stories about other family members, but keep from doing so, in fear that I would disapprove. It would all be too uncomfortable. I would be like a duck out of water."

"Are you sure you are not thinking of turkeys, instead of ducks?" I asked with a smile. I was enjoying this moment of awkwardness in Lodge. But I did not want to gloat. "The family would be delighted if you could join them. They are always asking about you. They would be thrilled."

"I wouldn't be imposing?"

"Of course not."

"Good," he said quickly. "I will come."

Thanksgiving arrived, and so did Lodge—promptly at noon, the appointed time. I had driven down the night before, to be able to help with preparations in the morning. Once Lodge appeared, I became more confused than ever, wondering why he had changed his habits and preferences so drastically. Why had he broken his monastic habit of celebrating Thanksgiving—as well as Christmas and Easter—alone?

His behavior provided me with no clue whatsoever. I had feared that he would just sit in a corner and sulk, absorbed in his own train of thought, but he did nothing of the sort. Quite the contrary, he revealed a side of himself I had never witnessed before—charming, engaging, and highly personable. If the only Lodge you ever met was the person on show that year at Thanksgiving, you would completely misread his character. He was the embodiment of everyone's mythical favorite uncle. He flattered my mother, presenting her with a bouquet of flowers that was rapidly transformed into a centerpiece for the table. He traded culinary secrets—mind you, I had never once seen him boil so much as an egg in my years of working with him—with her as she fussed over the gravy. He played chess with my father, diplomatically allowing him to make several brilliant moves that ended in mate, then engaged in small talk with Fay and May, even though May seemed giddier than usual. He admired Fay's children, who were running about inciting riot, being anything but adorable. He talked politics with Fay's husband Joe and with May's boyfriend Jeremy, even to the extreme of soliciting their opinions, which were as half-formed and bigoted as usual. I knew he could not care one whit for their opinions, and yet he remained cheerful and respectful in his conversations with them. He did not once chide them for their "thin-mindedness," as they surely deserved.

At dinner, he graciously accepted an invitation to offer the Thanksgiving prayer, which he boomed forth in grand stentorian style, ending with the dramatic flourish: "We all have so much more to be thankful for than we can possibly realize, as You share Your Abundance with us. Amen."

After helping himself to the turkey and sweet potatoes, he then reluctantly agreed to talk about his work in Thought Detection, captivating us all as he told tale after tale of mischief and mayhem—even stories I had not heard. He was the life of the party.

That evening, as we sat in the drawing room back in town, recovering from too much to be thankful for, he dropped the first clue. "I don't think your sister should marry that fellow she dragged home with her," he announced suddenly, definitively, and absolutely. The pope could not have spoken with more authority.

"I wasn't aware that May was even thinking of marriage—at least not any more than any other girl her age," I replied.

"Oh, she's definitely thinking of it," Lodge assured me. "Couldn't you tell? They are secretly engaged, and are planning to be married within two weeks. She was almost bursting with her secret."

That explained the giddiness, which I had chalked off as her reaction to being with the great Lodge. "The devil you say!" I stammered in utter amazement.

"I am surprised, Morgan, that you were so oblivious to the obvious clues. I must confess that I have never met your sister before, but I would venture to say that she is normally a mildly unpleasant person to be around: sharp of tongue, self-absorbed, and constantly expressing envy in lieu of admiration for others."

I had to admit he was correct.

"Yet she did not behave in any of these ways today. She was sweet and affectionate, even patient, not just toward Jeremy but everyone."

"Perhaps she was just on her good behavior today for a change—in honor of our distinguished guest, for example," I added, with as much sarcasm as I could lay on. Lodge chose to ignore my jab completely.

"Possible, but not likely. She is not that

skilled in covering up her true temperament. Morgan, she was actually radiating affection. Some women do that all of the time, of course, but there is one condition in which virtually all women do it—when they are engaged to be married. Once the proposal is made and accepted, the commitment starts to form at the emotional level, and the auras of both individuals become filled with the affection of their beloved, temporarily masking out their less noble qualities. It doesn't last for long, of course, but it is a genuine effect of being in love."

"That makes sense. But there is something that doesn't," I said.

"What is that?" asked Lodge.

"Why you are so interested in my sister's secrets," I replied.

"Ah, of course," Lodge said. "Well, that is simple, my friend. Jeremy is going to be arrested for murder within six weeks' time. I would hate to have her—and your family—dragged into a sordid mess by dint of an unfortunate alliance."

I was stunned. Flabbergasted might be the better word. "Murder?" I squeaked out meekly. "Why on earth would you suspect Jeremy of murder?"

"Did you ever read Nathaniel Hawthorne's *The Scarlet Letter*?"

"Of course."

"Well, murderers are branded pretty much the same way, although it is not with a scarlet 'A.' Murder is stamped all over Jeremy's character, if you know what you are looking for."

"How did my sister get hooked up with him? I mean, she's not always the most pleasant person on the planet, but she doesn't strike me as a murderer's consort, either."

"She's not," Lodge confirmed, "which is precisely why I have involved myself in this affair. She needs to learn better manners, but she deserves a happier fate than old Jeremy would provide. She needs to drop him—the sooner the better."

"But how?" I asked.

"Precisely. How indeed? If I tried to talk sense into her, she would just laugh and tell me to mind my own business—and rightly so. If you try to do the same, the results will be even worse—you will just drive her more defiantly into his arms."

"Is there no hope, then?" I inquired.

"There is always hope," Lodge said. "We must be willing to wait until she falls."

"Falls?"

"Falls out of love," Lodge amplified.

"Is that apt to happen?" I asked.

"I can almost guarantee it," Lodge said with

a conspiratorial smirk. "I just want you to be ready to catch her when it happens."

"Of course."

"Don't give into any brotherly urges to encourage her to stay in the relationship. We don't need that."

"Heavens no. But Lodge—"

"What?"

"If Jeremy is going to commit murder, why not just arrest him now, and save the life of whoever his victim might be?"

"I can't have a fellow arrested who has yet to commit a crime, Morgan. Even you know that. Besides, this will be a crime of impulse. He has no idea he is the murdering type—not yet, anyway."

"Well, there ought to be something you could do."

"I suppose there could be. But I am not inclined to interfere."

"Why on earth not?"

Lodge set down the glass of brandy he had been sipping. He looked me sternly in the eye. "Because his intended victim deserves to be killed. He has committed murder himself many times over."

"Has Jeremy?"

"Not many times, just once. In his last lifetime—and in cold blood. Once again, he has let a tremendous amount of anger and rage at life itself build up within his character. He is—what do you call it?—a walking time bomb of hostility waiting to explode. And this time bomb is magnetically drawing him into the very conditions that can cause him to detonate. He is drawing this murder to himself as surely as if he had hooked a fish on a line. I am not in a position to prevent it."

I was deeply troubled by Lodge's last statement, and his apparently cavalier regard for an event as monstrous as murder. Yet my regard for Lodge was so high that I refused to believe that he was either indifferent or callous. I trusted that he knew something about this case that I did not. His last words, "I am not in a position to prevent it," haunted me for days.

As predicted, my sister fell out of love with Jeremy—rather precipitously, in fact. One week after Thanksgiving, I got a call from her. May was crying. I could scarcely make out over the telephone what she was trying to say. It seems Jeremy had just humiliated her in front of a group of friends—at a party—by relating to them secrets she had told him in confidence. When she asked him to stop, he laughed cruelly and then continued on. "He was so mean," she sobbed. She told him it was over and left the party. He made no effort to follow.

But now she was unhappy, and wanted me to encourage her to return to him. "No way," I said. "You deserve better than Jeremy. Don't ever give him a chance to hurt you like that again. Trust me—you are far better off without him."

She did not welcome my advice with open arms—but she did accept it.

All that night, I lay awake wondering. How had Lodge known my sister would break up with Jeremy? How did he know she would try to use me to convince her to go back to him?

The answer came to me in a flash. There in the dark, at 3 in the morning, give or take an hour, I said a heartfelt prayer. It was a prayer for my sister, but not just my sister. It was a prayer for every victim of Jeremy's cruelty and rage. It was a prayer for Jeremy—for all of the Jeremy's of the world.

I cannot say that it was a good prayer, in any way. I learned a number of stock prayers as a child, of course, but none of them seemed to fit the circumstances. At 3 o'clock in the morning, however, form does not seem as important as it may at other times. I just tried to pray from the heart.

I prayed that my sister May be protected from any further romantic thoughts about Jeremy. I prayed that Jeremy's intended victim be spared the fatal assault of his cruelty and anger. I prayed that Jeremy's conscience grow as strong as it possibly could, to insulate him from his own dark, criminal moods. I prayed for the best for everyone involved in this sordid mess. I prayed in the silence and in the darkness, invoking the silence to lift me out of the darkness. I was answered by silence and light. I think I also smelled a faint trace of crabapple, and sensed an approving nod, somewhere in the distant night. And then, utterly exhausted, I fell asleep.

One month later, Jeremy was arraigned in court for manslaughter. He had killed a man in a barroom brawl—a man who had insinuated quite loudly that Jeremy was gay. Jeremy had demanded an apology, and his antagonist had taken a swing at him. Jeremy had then shoved the man against the bar and let go of him. As the man fell, his head struck the brass railing, knocking him unconscious.

"I thought you said he would be arrested for murder," I said to Lodge when I first got the news—from May. "Why was it only manslaughter?"

Lodge looked at me with his penetrating stare, but I detected the same sense of approval I had felt a month before, when I fell asleep praying. "It seems I was careless in speech," he said slowly, mitering each word for maximum impact. "Someone took it upon himself to intrude into matters that did not involve him, thus changing the anticipated outcome.

"When I first became aware of Jeremy, a week before Thanksgiving, it was clear to me that he would be arrested for murder after burning down the bar in which this incident occurred. His victim, whom he had just knocked unconscious, would be lying on the floor of the bar, unable to move. Realizing he was in great trouble, Jeremy would flee. On his way out, he would trip and fall in an alley next to the bar. As he got back on his feet, he would see a discarded cigarette lighter and some old boxes. In a panic, he would ignite the boxes and burn down the bar. Everyone inside would escape—except his unconscious victim. It would be a fair compensation for the victim, however, for the fellow had roasted any number of innocent people at the stake during the heyday of the Inquisition.

"Jeremy would be identified by the owner of the bar, and traces of accelerant from the lighter would be found on his clothing. He would be arrested for murder, tried and convicted, and sent to the chair.

"On the night of the actual incident, all of the elements were in place as I had originally envisioned. As Jeremy stormed out of the bar, having leveled his antagonist with one swing, he saw the lighter and contemplated arson. His anger was still explosive; he stood for a moment in the balance, swaying to and fro between arson and fleeing. In the final, fateful moment, he swayed a bit more toward the best within him than to his anger, and he dropped the lighter and fled.

"Inside the tavern, the bartender called 911; an emergency rescue team came and tried to revive the unconscious man. But they were not successful—he died en route to the hospital."

"Incidentally, Morgan, you will be interested to know that even though Jeremy has been arrested for manslaughter, he will be acquitted. His lawyer will successfully plead self-defense. There is even a chance he may have learned his lesson—at least about murdering."

"But why didn't you foresee this outcome?"

"I couldn't have," replied Lodge. "It wasn't known at the time."

"Why not?"

"Isn't it obvious?" Lodge replied. "You had not yet said your prayers."

Eight

An Overture To Death

"Are you a magnet for bizarre deaths, Lodge?" We were standing in the upscale apartment of Donald Fester, an acclaimed musicologist who had just hours before hummed his last melody. He lay very dead on the floor, a look of obscene horror frozen permanently on his face. And yet, to all appearances, Fester had died of natural causes. It had not yet been determined that he had been murdered.

Thought detective Walter J. Lodge chuckled at the question, which had been directed at him by his friend, the mayor. "There is a very old principle, Jack," he responded, "which states that energy follows attention. Since the only reason why you ever call on me is to help you solve the crime du jour, it naturally appears to you that I attract bizarre deaths. But it must be you who has the magnetism, since *you* call *me*—not the other way around."

His Honor affected to squirm. "Ouch!" he said with playful realism. "I think you hooked me on that one."

Corinna Caxton, our district attorney, was interested in other issues. "What do you think of our dead friend here, Lodge? Is it a natural death—or is it murder?"

"Both, I am afraid," replied Lodge coolly. "But what made you even suspect the possibility of foul play? There is no suggestion of it here—no sign of a struggle, no poison in the wine glasses. Except for the horror of the death mask, the deceased would seem to have died of an ordinary heart attack or stroke."

The police chief stepped into the circle. He was a chubby man with a bright red face. Lodge always referred to him—outside his hearing—as Chester, for reasons I never have fathomed. The man's name was actually Adam Goodman. "Fester was entertaining a guest when he died. We first learned about it when the guest came running into the precinct office panting, 'I killed him. I killed him.' "

" 'Killed whom?' the desk sergeant asked.

" 'My friend,' the man replied. 'I have killed my friend. I don't know how, but I did it. That's all I know. I killed him.'

"Upon questioning, we decided the man was a bit hysterical. It seems he was visiting the deceased, an old friend of his, for the first time in some twenty years. The man had studied music with Fester years ago, and had become quite an accomplished pianist. But he had spent most of the last twenty years on the continent. This was his first trip back. Fester asked him to play something for him on the piano. The friend was halfway through when Fester cried out, 'No! No!' He staggered toward the piano as if to stop the music, then fell forward, dead, with that horrible look on his face."

"Do you have this guest in custody?" Lodge asked.

"Not custody, as such," Chief Goodman responded. "We thought he needed some mental attention—some help in calming himself down and accepting the death of his friend."

"Friend?" Lodge repeated. He betrayed a brief look of revulsion at the prospect, then let his eyes stare far, far before him. I recognized the stare easily enough. He was looking down the halls of time. Then he abruptly snapped out of it. "May I interview the guest?"

Goodman sent for the man. In the ten or fifteen minutes it took to drive him from the police station, I surveyed the scene of the crime. There were two wine glasses. One was set neatly on the top ledge of the piano, still half filled with wine. The other was lying, its contents spilled, on the carpet next to the dead body. Judging from the nearly empty bottle by one of the chairs, they had been enjoying an expensive bottle of imported French wine—a *Chateauneuf du Pape*, in fact, estate bottled. Everything else in the room apparently lay exactly where it was that morning, before anything happened. I wandered briefly through the other rooms in the apartment, but they yielded no clues. They told me nothing.

When the mysterious guest arrived, he was still shaking visibly from his ordeal. Lodge welcomed him cordially and asked him to sit down. The sight of the corpse of Donald Fester, still lying on the floor, almost sent him into hysteria again, but he managed to control himself.

Lodge set him at ease in a matter of moments, however. He started by asking his name.

"My name is Gerald Bookman," the man said quietly. "I am a pianist. I live in Vienna."

"Yes, I know," replied Lodge. "I own several of your recordings. I am particularly fond of your performance of C.P.E. Bach's sonatas. I thought you transferred them from the harpsichord to the piano with great deftness."

Bookman looked up at Lodge. "You know my work?"

"A tremendous depth of sensitivity," Lodge amplified, "although I sometimes think you are a better interpreter of the darkness within human nature than of our potential for joy and wisdom. I would prefer more of the latter."

"Right now, I would, too," Bookman moaned, disconsolately. "I feel as though I have sunk into the dark hole of human nature and been swallowed up by the night—piano and all."

Lodge acknowledged his predicament.

"Tell me, if you will, how you knew Donald Fester?"

Bookman drew in a deep breath. "I am a pianist. Donald was a professor of mine at university. He admired my technique tremendously, and of course I admired his musical knowledge and sensitivity. There was a strong bond between us from the day I first met him, although we never spoke of it. I always assumed it was our mutual love of music. Tonight, I am not so sure." He turned and looked at Lodge. "Could music kill a man?" he asked, almost desperately.

"That's what we are trying to find out," Lodge replied.

"I have been performing for years in Europe, primarily in Germany and Austria. I am as well known in Vienna as Jean Paul Rampal is in this country. A few months ago, I had a sudden desire to return to the states and visit my old friend Donald Fester. It became an overwhelming urge that had to be obeyed. I called him and asked if everything was all right; I was afraid that perhaps he was dying. He assured me that he was in wonderful health, and had no intention of 'checking out,' as he put it, but invited me to come see him most emphatically. 'We shall have a grand time,' he said, adding, 'be sure to bring me any quaint tunes you have picked up in Vienna.'

"I arrived yesterday. Once I had checked into my hotel, I called Donald to let him know I had arrived. He insisted I come over right away—which I did. We talked awhile, catching up on each other's careers, drinking some wine. Then he asked me what delicious tunes I had brought from the Alps to entertain him.

" 'I hope you have something I have never heard before,' he said eagerly.

"I told him I had recently uncovered a tune that had been written originally for the harpsichord some two hundred and fifty years ago. I was completely enthralled by it the moment I first heard it. I immediately memorized and then transcribed it for the piano.

"Donald insisted that I play it for him without further delay, poured us each a fresh glass of wine, and then sat down with a tremendous smile of anticipation on his face.

"But as I began playing, I noticed that he was becoming alarmed, even though my performance seemed inspired—I might even say, 'elevated.' I kept on playing, but the darkness on his brow grew stronger. I came to the climax of the first part, and suddenly he stood up and shouted, 'No, no!' It was as though he were possessed. Then he collapsed dead on the floor. I tried to revive him, but he was stone-cold dead.

"Having been out of the country for all of these years, I did not know about your emergency system. So I rushed out of the apartment to find some help. There was none around. I just started running down the street, until I found the precinct office. I went in and told my story."

"But why did you cry, 'I killed him; I killed him'?" Lodge asked.

"I do not know," Bookman replied. "It just seems perfectly clear to me that I did. I did not touch him in any way, but somehow the music I was playing killed him. There is no other possible explanation, even though this one seems utterly absurd."

"I agree," Lodge said. "I agree that your music killed him—and I also agree that it seems completely absurd. But I am afraid that it is not."

"Can you explain what that means?" asked Chief Goodman.

"I have not yet made all of the connections myself," Lodge replied, "but I think I have discerned enough of the truth to sketch out the outline of the story. The details will probably fall into place as I talk." He walked over to the piano and began playing. It was a haunting melody, almost sad, but filled with a tremendous power. For a moment, I thought that Gerald was going to die, too, but he merely staggered backwards and sat down in a chair, keeping his eyes transfixed on Lodge at the same time.

Lodge approached a climax, and then abruptly stopped. "Is this the point where Donald Fester died?" he asked.

"Y-y-y-yes," the guest stammered. "But how do you know this song—and how can you play it so well? You have duplicated my phrasing precisely. It was an amazing performance!"

Lodge smiled sadly, a thin, piteous smile. "It's all in the mind," he said. "The being you knew as Donald Fester is standing here beside the piano, explaining the events. Until the moment he died, he did not fully recognize the song you played—even though it was he who had composed it in an earlier lifetime, almost three hundred years ago."

"What?" chorused Bookman, Chief Goodman, Corinna Caxton, and Jack in unison.

"He tells me he lived in a remote part of Germany and played the organ for the local church. A plague swept through the village, killing many parishioners. He was moved to write this piece of music, which he entitled 'An Overture to Death.'"

"So? How is that connected with his death today?"

"By itself, it is not," Lodge proceeded. "But Fester's link with death was nothing new.

"Centuries before, in a much earlier lifetime, he had been a military officer who led raids on neighboring towns. In one instance," Lodge said, turning to the guest, "he sacked and looted a town where you, in a different body, lived with your family. Your parents were slaughtered, and Fester himself took your sister, raped her, and then disemboweled her—for his own sick pleasure. He made you watch, then killed you as well. But before you died, you swore to exact vengeance upon him, and you damned his soul to hell. Fester responded by taunting your inability to take revenge as he slit your throat. You died spitting your own blood in his face."

Bookman hung his head sorrowfully. "I

wish I could say I have no idea what you are talking about. But I do. As Fester started to collapse, I felt a strange force seizing me. I am often lifted up by wonderful forces of harmony and beauty when I am truly at one with my music, but this was completely different. I felt the vengeance surge through my veins and my breath. It drove me to play the music even more vigorously and stridently. I feel as though I pounded the life out of Donald Fester right there on the keyboard."

"I know," Lodge said quietly. He turned to the rest of us.

"For the record, Donald Fester was murdered from within. He choked on the venom of his own guilt. But he was helped along by the visit of his old friend Gerald Bookman—and by the very funeral dirge Fester had composed more than two centuries ago. He wrote it, even then, in anticipation of his own murder."

"I hope you are planning to clarify that statement, Walter," Jack said.

"I expect to," Lodge replied. He paused to gather his thoughts.

"Vengeance is the nastiest of all human emotions, birthed out of hatred and nursed on gall. It squeezes the life out of anyone who embraces it—and forces them into strange, intimate, but unholy bonds with the persons they hate.

"In this case, the lust for revenge dates back thousands of years, when Fester was a tribal war lord in Asia. Through me, Fester has already described the unspeakable acts he committed in his ignorance and arrogance. The bond that has linked the two of these people for all of this time, however, was forged not by Fester but by the frightened lad who saw his sister brutalized by a foreigner.

"The link of vengeance has united the two of them ever since that village raid. Bookman has actually had innumerable opportunities to settle the score in these intervening years, but he could not bring himself to do so. He did not want to have to confront the need to forgive Fester—and if he ever evened the score, that is what he was going to have to do. He preferred to torture and harass Fester, than to give up his hatred.

"But the benevolence of life cannot be mocked. Gradually, Bookman began to recognize the evolving humanity within Fester, especially his musical talents and gifts. None of us ever stands still, and Donald Fester did not remain a barbaric warlord. He paid the price for his hatred, and became a civilized human being. Still linked by Gerald's vengeance, they nonetheless became admirers—and friends. It was always an uneasy friendship, to be sure—a "wary one" might be a better way to describe it. But believe it or not, the power of friendship gradually became as strong as—and then even stronger than—the power of vengeance.

"Unfortunately, the vengeance did not diminish, and Bookman continued to be unwilling to forgive. So fate arranged to have Fester write the 'Overture to Death,' just weeks before he himself died of the plague. The piece contains an intricate musical code which triggered memories of horror and vengeance—for both of the men—as they listened to it.

"This is the reason why Gerald established his career in Vienna, instead of in this country. He needed to be in the right place to 'discover' the long forgotten piece when the time was ripe.

"He came back triumphantly to his friend the musicologist, having found a musical treasure for his enjoyment. But it was a lethal gift. As Gerald sat here playing"—and Lodge began to play the song again—"the whole scenario of what had happened surged into Fester's awareness from deep wells of consciousness within him. He remembered writing "An Overture to Death"—and knew instantly it was now being played for him. He then remembered the panoply of lives in which he had tormented his friend and in which his friend had pursued him with vengeance. He tried to deny the power of Fate by crying out, 'No! No!' But it was to no avail. The coils of vengeance had wrapped around him like a boa constrictor, and as they twisted, he writhed, until he died of hallucinatory suffocation. This accounts for the look of absolute horror on his face."

Lodge turned to the guest, who was sobbing. "Will you end it now?"

"Can I?" he replied.

"Absolutely," Lodge answered. "You can end it by forgiving Donald Fester, and by forswearing vengeance from this day forward. It has made a slave of you—and you have served lifetime after lifetime in servitude to it. Are you weary of it at last?"

Once more, Bookman's "yes" was barely audible, but he said it.

Lodge looked pleased. "I am glad. Otherwise, the vengeance would have driven you completely mad. And the world would have lost an inspired pianist."

"The world has lost Donald Fester, and I am responsible for it," the man sobbed.

"No," Lodge replied. "You are not. Fester

is standing before you, telling us all that he wanted to be released from his murderous deeds as much as you are glad to be rid of your lust for revenge. It seems to me that you are both well served by these events, and will now be able to be good friends in the future without having to worry about being betrayed.

"As for the resolution of this case," said Lodge, turning to Chief Goodman, Ms. Caxton, the mayor, and me, "I recommend that the case be ruled as a death by natural causes and closed. There are not many emotions in the human armory more natural than vengeance—nor more deadly."

Nine

An Overdose of Bad History

"Will Short was a victim of a biased, corrupt educational system—our public schools." These were the first words Walter J. Lodge had uttered since stepping into the city hall office of Will Short. Will had died a week earlier. There were no signs of foul play. The autopsy had revealed no cause of death. Yet it seemed unreasonable to believe that a 37-year-old man had died of natural causes while in his office at work. The mayor and the chief of police both suspected "unnatural causes."

Will had been an energetic member of the mayor's staff; I had worked "in the trenches" with him on several political campaigns. He knew his stuff, and it was not just great instincts. He was an educated man; he could have passed for a professor in most crowds. I had always admired the depth of his thought, and his ability to take on any debate, on any subject, and win it. He was the nimblest thinker I knew—other than Lodge, of course, who was in a class by himself.

The mayor had asked Lodge to come to city

hall to investigate. Walter J. Lodge is a friend of the mayor; he has consulted with Jack on numerous crimes. Lodge is a "thought detective"—he uses only his mind to solve strange and bizarre crimes. I work with him, as his assistant. I had witnessed many unusual things in the years since I had joined forces with Lodge. I had heard things even more strange. But I do not believe I had ever heard anything quite so unexpected as the announcement that Will Short had been killed by our public school system!

"What do you mean?" asked the mayor.

Lodge turned to his old friend. "I mean, Jack, that he was killed by an overdose of bad history." He turned to Adam Goodman, the chief of police. "Your men will find all of the evidence right here," Lodge said, tapping the computer that was still sitting on Will's old desk. "He kept notes—notes that will collaborate what I am about to tell you."

Chief Goodman called in forensic experts who started "hacking" the computer to download its files and sift through them. Lodge proceeded to tell the story as he had perceived it mentally:

"Like everyone else attending our public schools in the last fifty years, Will Short was taught more misinformation about human history than correct information. Like everyone else, he believed what he was taught—and based his values, morals, and attitudes toward life upon those facts."

"I am not sure I am following you." Jack interrupted. "What kind of misinformation?"

"Just about everything under the sun. We have been taught that the Western Hemisphere was originally populated by Asians crossing a hypothetical land bridge between Siberia and Alaska, then working their way methodically down to the tip of Cape Horn. We have been taught that the European settlers of this country inflicted genocide on the native American population. We have been taught that only the white race ever owned black slaves. We have been taught that capitalism is bad and evil and that communism is the salvation of 'the people.' We have been taught that successful business people are exploiters of their employees and enemies of the environment. We have been taught that freedom of speech means that we must never say anything that might offend anyone else."

"Aren't those things true?" I asked. "Other than communism being good, of course."

"Ah, I see you were bitten by the same bug, Morgan," Lodge replied. "I have neglected to help you update your education. There is a germ of truth in these facts, of course. But they fail to convey the whole picture of history.

"The Western Hemisphere has been inhabited for hundreds of thousands of years, since the days of Lemuria, a civilization that flourished in the Pacific Ocean basin. Parts of the hemisphere were also inhabited during the heydey of Atlantis. When Atlantis collapsed about 15,000 years ago, many groups of people fled westward, settling in New England, in Virginia, in the Mayan peninsula, and in Peru, just as some groups fled eastward, to Egypt, the Middle East, Greece, and elsewhere. The Americas have been populated a long, long time."

"But isn't that just speculation and myth?" asked Jack.

"The speculative part is what they are teaching in school. The only historical record we have on the subject is Plato's references to Atlantis. And yet historians reject the one reference they actually have in favor of unadulterated supposititon. The problem is they do not label it 'speculation.' They treat it as fact.

"Facts can be used to prove just about anything, you know. If the European settlers engaged in genocide, how is it possible that the Indian population in this country is larger today than when the European settlers first came? And did you know that southern Indians owned black slaves just as the white settlers around them did? We are taught about robber barons and led to believe that all capitalists make all their money by stealing it—but we are not taught that communism has failed to create a sustainable economy in any country in which it has governed. We are never taught that communist rulers purge their opponents by executing them, repress all religion, and treat their citizens as though they were heads of cabbage.

"In recent years, the problem of bad history has gotten even worse. History books devote three pages to the struggles of Betsy Ross sewing the first flag, but dismiss the life and contributions of General George Washington in three sentences! In fact, bad history is beginning to pollute other subjects in our schools as well. We now teach bad science as well, especially in politically sensitive areas such as the environment. We are taught about the destructive impact of humanity—but not taught that Mother Earth has enormous recuperative powers of her own. The whole process is being corrupted by sophists.

"Will first became aware of the problem of bad history about a half a year ago. While working on a project here at city hall, he came across some old writings about the early days of this city. He discovered that Indians in this part of the country were never the targets of any kind of "ethnic cleansing," as is commonly taught in our elementary schools now. For the most part, in fact, they lived peaceably and cooperatively with their white neighbors. One Indian was the first real capitalist in this area two hundred years ago, and is actually responsible for the founding of the city. He built a ferry across the river and a trading post on this side. As travellers passed through, back and forth along the trade routes, his trading post began to draw other commerce. A thriving metropolis of one million people is the result of one Indian's success as a capitalist. "

"I actually knew that," said Jack.

Lodge laughed. "Sure. You are the mayor of the city where it happened. But do you think kids in Ohio read about it? Not a chance."

"Will began exploring other topics. He found out he had been misinformed on lots of subjects. One that caught his attention is the phony schism between labor and management—a non-existent conflict dreamed up by Karl Marx and perpetuated by one hundred years of labor activists. The truth of the matter is that labor and management are not only dependent upon each other, but have exactly the same goals. Labor needs management to provide jobs. Management needs labor to get the work done. They both need a strong company to preserve their prosperity. So where is the alleged conflict? It only exists in the minds of those who believe in it. It is a concept that has no more validity than the idea of a flat earth.

"As a result of all this research, Will began to think. He imitated Descartes in a campaign that began with doubting everything, and then started focusing on what he knew to be true. He taught himself to think for himself. He questioned everything he read in the papers—not just the slant, which many people can see, but the actual truthfulness of the "facts" as they are presented. He questioned the lack of real thinking in political agendas. He questioned everything—but without rejecting anything! He was smart enough to realize that it was not history that was at fault, but our tendency to reinterpret history to suit modern fancy.

"A person who begins to think discovers all kinds of truths that had been hidden by bias and superstition before. It was an exciting time for Will. He knew he was onto something big. He plunged into his mental investigations even more vigorously.

"This, unfortunately, made him a danger. There are certain forces in our human family who prosper mightily by keeping people ill-informed. They have worked very hard to train the masses to accept what they are told through blind belief. They do not like it when someone like Will begins thinking. One thinking person can easily awaken a hundred or even a thousand more thinkers. It is a tremendous blow to these dark forces to let anyone learn to think, even a political operative like Will Short.

"So, they killed him."

"How?" I asked, incredulous.

"How indeed?" chimed in Jack.

"At first, they tried to drive him to suicide. Many suicides are actually a form of mental murder. If one person hates another devotedly for thirty or forty years, it may do so much damage that the hated party may end up killing himself. But the damage done to the hater is even greater, and he usually commits suicide shortly after his victim does. It is not out of remorse, unfortunately; it is the result of not having his victim around any more to hate! It has become such an integral part of life that life is no longer worth living.

"The type of suicidal thoughts that were targeted at Will is even more rare. While he was in the phase of doubting everything, his attackers tried—unsuccessfully—to increase the 'volume' of his doubt to unbearable levels, hoping he would kill himself in despair. But Will had already established a strong enough baseline of ethics and principles to deflect any such suggestions. He knew what he stood for and had firm values that protected him from committing suicide. Remember what I said a few moments ago about 'not rejecting anything for its own sake'? That is precisely what kept him alive.

"So they had to resort to a more insidious method."

"And what was that?" I asked. I could see myself in poor Will's position very easily.

"Pure, undiluted hate. He was basically frozen to death. But by the time anyone discovered him, all signs of the method had disappeared."

"I don't understand," said Chief Goodman.

"And that is good," said Lodge. "If you understood, you would be susceptible to the same kind of attack yourself. Will Short understood, so he had to be eliminated.

"Basically, Will was encased in very strong hatred for about six hours. During that time, his temperature was methodically lowered by mental means to a level that could no longer support life. He froze. But once he was dead, the attack withdrew, and his temperature returned to normal levels—normal for a dead man."

"Wasn't he able to fight it?" the chief of police asked.

"At first, he had no idea what was happening to him," Lodge replied. "He felt horribly cold, but he interpreted his problem entirely on an emotional level—the level of hatred. And he inverted the attack—a very common response. He misread the hatred that was filling him and thought it was his own. He began to recall anyone and everything he had even the slightest grudge against, and mistakenly assumed this hatred was his own repressed feeling toward them. He assumed that this rising level of anger and animosity within him was the byproduct of his own explorations of the mind. Only too late did he realize what was actually happening, as he began to get glimpses of his tormentor. But by then he was on the verge of losing consciousness. He could not fight."

"Do you know who did this unspeakable thing?" asked the mayor.

"Absolutely," said Lodge. "I would recognize his involvement anywhere I found it."

"It's a living person?" I asked.

"To be sure."

"Can you name him?" asked the mayor, then hesitated before adding: "and would I recognize his name?"

"I could—and you would," replied Lodge evenly. "but do you want me to name him? Could you live with the knowledge? Or would it expose you to the same fate Will Short suffered?"

"Is there any way to bring him to justice?"

"Not until there is a law against murder by mind," Lodge answered. "The man in question was more than one hundred miles distant at the time Will died, by the way. And he was not the only one involved. He had a small band of followers who helped him do the dirty deed."

"Could we arrest him on other charges?" asked the mayor.

"You could arrest him on thousands of counts," Lodge replied. "But I doubt that any of them would stick. It would be awfully hard to find a court that would accept jurisdiction for conspiracy to murder Thomas à Becket—even if you could prove the case."

"So what do we do—just ignore Will Short's demise?"

"No, we leave our villain to divine law. The mental plane is patrolled by a kind of God

Squad, and the laws of divine life are enforced meticulously. Our villain will be consumed by his own hate, well before the end of this lifetime. He will not commit suicide—he is too well disciplined for that—but he will be eliminated by a jealous colleague."

We parted company with the mayor, who had a function to attend. On our way back home, I asked the obvious but unspoken question:

"Aren't you in danger of being murdered, Lodge? You are certainly more of a threat to such a person than Will Short ever was!"

"Ah, but I know what I am doing. They have tried to kill me—many times. But if you are able to protect yourself, you learn from every attempt. Soon, you build up a strong immunity. They have basically given up trying to kill me, except for the occasional token scare. They know they are not going to be able to succeed."

"But how did you survive the initial attempts, when poor Will Short did not?"

"Easy, Morgan. I work as part of a group. Will Short did not realize that he could tap such support. He was just a random individual who started using his mind—and broke through to the truth.

"It's sad, actually. He was given the chance

to come work with us, and be trained by me. There was a case not long ago—the case of the woman in blue, I believe—where the mayor asked Will to come pick us up and meet him at the crime scene. Jack did not know the larger ramifications of that request, but it was intended to bring Will into contact with me. I would have done the rest. But Will begged off, saying he was not feeling well—which was true. So the contact was never made. I dare say the symptoms of not feeling well were a well-focused pre-emptory strike from the dark forces to keep Will from making contact with me. Well, it worked.

"Will was completely unprepared for the assault from the forces that do not want people to think—and never even suspected it. When the onslaught came, he had no way to align himself to the power of any group that might protect him. He was an easy mark—although he will not be in future lives. He has learned his lesson—and a valuable one it will be, too.

"In fact, it is Will who has been filling me in on most of the details of the case. He is very much alive, even though his physical body died. He does not regret having taken these risks—or losing the battle. He knows he has taken a big step in winning the war.

"This is why I approach every case impersonally, though. If I took a personal interest, I would be exposing myself to attack. Instead, I work on behalf of a small group of thinking people. Whenever I am attacked, the whole group rallies to my aid.

"What if the group could not handle the attack?"

"That is not a possibility. The group has a decided advantage. The ones who try to keep people from thinking can attack only our feelings and our thoughts. So they try to make someone like Will very depressed or overwhelmed—or militantly doubtful and arrogant. The group I belong to is focused at higher levels—in principles and patterns. These principles and patterns cannot be corrupted or diminished in any way, even by hate. So we always win, as long as we remained absorbed in virtue."

"Virtue?" I asked.

"Yes, virtue," said Lodge. "The infinite power of God."

"I don't know," I said. "I think it's all over my head."

"Actually, Morgan," Lodge said mischievously. "It's all in the mind."

Ten

Miranda's Rights

I awoke in the middle of the night, surrounded by terror. It was not my terror, even though I could feel it and sense it as clearly as if the room were filled with smoke or perfume. It was the terror of someone being burned to death. It was most unsettling, but I knew it was not my problem, nor my worry. So I went back to sleep—a very fitful sleep, I am afraid, not restful at all. I was still plagued by the unsettling feeling of being burned alive when I arose in the morning.

At breakfast, I mentioned my experience to Lodge, and asked if he had perceived the same wave of terror.

"No," he responded, "I slept quite soundly all night." He had another bite of a cranberry scone. "But remember, your quarters are in the carriage house, not here in the main house. So there might be no connection at all between what you and I might happen to experience during the night."

He paused to reflect on the situation. "The Gentleman"—Lodge's name for the man who had originally built the mansion, "is telling me that a chauffeur in his employ died in a fire in your quarters seventy-five years ago. He fell asleep smoking a cigarette, and did not awaken in time to save himself. But he did awaken in time to experience a few seconds of unmitigated horror. I imagine you tuned into a memory of that experience while asleep."

"Why did I happen to perceive his horror last night?"

"Significant energy patterns of strong emotion or thought tend to cling to the walls of a building for many years without dissipating." Lodge explained. "You tuned into those patterns like a radio tuning into a specific station on the dial."

"But why had I not tuned in earlier?" I asked. "How long have I lived here now? It must be four or five years."

"Something has happened that magnified the importance of this particular feeling, and brought it to your attention," Lodge replied. "My guess is that it is some kind of advance clue to a case that will be developing soon."

"You mean I am being intuitive?" I asked.

"It's more a case of the carriage house being intuitive, my friend," Lodge laughed. "If you had been intuitive, you would have figured out the meaning of your experience without asking me."

Lodge had another bite of breakfast, then continued. "You were given the major clue you needed to work with: the pall of terror. You even correctly realized that it was not your terror, but someone else's, and that it was connected with fire and death. But there you stopped, instead of following the clues. Were they burned at the stake? No. Were they murdered by arson? No. Did they die at their own hand? Yes, but not as a suicide. Was it an accidental death? Where? Right in your own quarters! Q.E.D.!

"Always remember to follow the clues," Lodge concluded triumphantly.

"You make it seem so easy," I muttered.

"And it is," Lodge replied. "It's just a question of practice."

Perhaps it was the scone, but Lodge was warming up to the discussion. He was in an unusually loquacious mood.

"The Gentleman suggests that I explain to you some of the recent discoveries I have made in the house, with his assistance," Lodge began. "It will help you realize that not only can walls talk, but they are somehow alive—or at least in tune with a much larger living entity. The house is like a huge electric guitar."

I told Lodge he had lost me at the junction of "living entity" and "huge electric guitar."

"Well, then," Lodge said amiably. "Let me begin again. I have discovered that this house—the whole estate, in fact—was carefully laid out to take advantage of the earth's natural magnetic grid. The earth is not just a big ball of dirt and stone; it is an electrically charged orb. When you see lightning in the sky, you are often seeing it arc from the ground to the sky, rather than the other way around. This is because the earth is as electrically charged as the thunderheads, and the lightning is arcing back and forth between the two.

"Before building this house, the Gentleman had discovered that the earth was electrically charged, and had also realized that the charge is much stronger in some areas than in others. The energy of the earth tends to flow in currents much like rivers do. In fact, rivers and ravines tend to run along the same lines as many of these electrical pathways. In England, they call these pathways "ley lines." In the Orient, they call them "chi" and have made a whole science out of studying the impact of these energies on human life.

"The gentleman built his home in such a way that it is completely powered by the natural electricity of the earth!" Lodge continued.

"Instead of harnessing solar power or hydro power, he was able to harness the positive electrical charge of the earth itself, and was able to draw virtually unlimited reservoirs of it. In fact, he was able to generate more than he needed, so he fed the excess back to the electric company! He had a feed-in from the electric company, just like everyone else, until he discovered how to draw his power from the earth. The meter actually went backward instead of forward, and the electric company paid him each month for the electricity that they used—at full retail rates! The money he made in this fashion comprised a sizeable portion of his wealth."

"Are you still selling electricity to the utility company?" I asked.

"It hasn't worked out," Lodge replied. "The practice ceased when The Gentleman died. By the time I bought his mansion, none of the officers of the electric company that had known and dealt with The Gentleman were still alive. The current officers do not have the same level of imagination as they did. I suppose I could make a fuss about it, but I prefer to live quietly, not draw attention to myself. So I let it go.

"Besides, the most fascinating aspect of this house is one I am just learning about. Watch."

The kitchen lights suddenly dimmed, then went off.

"Count to three," Lodge said.

I counted three. The lights came back on.

"I am learning to blend my own energy field with the electrical system of the house, just as you blended your awareness with the pattern of fear left behind by the dying chaffeur. The only difference is that I can use this ability at will, and you cannot. It takes the utmost discipline, though, lest a careless word or thought short-circuit the entire system!

"I have learned to control almost every electrical function in the house just by thinking of the outcome I wish," Lodge proceeded. "Are you comfortable, Morgan?"

"I'm a little chilled, in fact."

"This should fix it," Lodge affirmed. He rested for a moment, his eyes fixed on a point that did not exist in the physical plane. A couple of seconds later, I heard the furnace come on, and warm air began pouring onto my feet.

"That's incredible!" I exclaimed. "Can you do it anywhere?"

"Perhaps," Lodge replied. "But it would be much more difficult. I have the advantage of working with a very much advanced electrical system here, as designed and built by The

Gentleman. Because it is plugged into the earth's electrical grid, it is easy to manipulate mentally. After all, the earth is intelligent, and so I am. It is a perfect match."

Lodge paused. "I would love to go on, but I think our services are required elsewhere. Jack is going to need us on a case. He won't realize that he needs us for a couple of days, if he's left to figure it out on his own. But we will be in a much better position to help if we show up now. If we leave for city hall now, we can intercept him just before he leaves the building."

I looked at Lodge. "Why don't we just go to the scene of the crime?"

"We would if I knew where it was," he smiled.

"I know where it is," I replied. "I do not know how I know, but I do."

"Hmmm," Lodge pondered. "What kind of crime is it?"

I smiled. "Arson, of course."

"You are well taught, Morgan," Lodge replied. "Well taught."

So we went to the scene, arriving a good ten minutes before the mayor—although not before the murder was actually committed. As we drove up, we saw the remains of a residential home, smoldering in ashes.

We were met by the chief of police, Adam Goodman.

"The body is in the kitchen, burnt beyond recognition," I said, surprising myself yet again.

"Hey," Goodman grunted, "I thought it was Lodge who came up with the mumbo-jumbo, and that you were the sane half of the team. What gives?"

"Damned if I know," I replied. "But I seem to be stocked with answers I know nothing about—until the questions arise."

Adam confirmed that they had found a body in the kitchen. It was about that time that the mayor, our friend Jack, arrived.

While Jack was receiving a briefing from the chief, Lodge started his intuitive investigations. I could tell from the subtle changes in his demeanor, his thoughtfulness, and his air of distraction. He was working in a different world than the rest of us.

"Well, Lodge, what do you think?" Jack asked, once he had been told the few facts that Goodman knew.

"It is a strange case," Lodge replied. "So far, the only substantial clue I have to follow is that Morgan is somehow connected with the crime. It may be that he knows the victim—or maybe the arsonist, I haven't been able to figure it out yet. He had a strong enough tie to draw us to the crime scene, but it does not seem to be a good enough connection to yield any further clues.

"Normally, the scene of the crime produces lots of clues. But since this murder was committed through arson, the fire has purged most of the tangible psychic clues that are usually left behind."

"Did you say 'murder'?" Adam asked. "Why do you think it is murder? We've been treating it as an ordinary fire. We have no reason to believe it was arson—or if there was any attempt to kill."

"Oh, it was murder," Lodge replied with certainty. "The man who died—his name is Sam—is standing right next to you, Chief, insisting it was murder. He has been trying to tell you this ever since you showed up a half an hour ago."

Goodman jumped a half step, as if to not get too close to the dead man's spirit.

Lodge continued. "Sam is showing me that someone—a woman—approached his house in the wee hours of the morning, doused a shrub near his front door with kerosene, then tossed a match on it. As the kerosene burst into flame and enveloped the front porch, she drove off. He woke up a few minutes later in sheer horror, flames dancing around his bed and spreading rapidly throughout the house. He got up and staggered to the kitchen, but he was overcome by smoke and collapsed. He died shortly thereafter."

"Does Sam know me?" I asked, trying to find a link that would explain my dream and ongoing rapport with this man.

"No." Lodge replied. "He has no idea what attracted you to this particular event."

"Can he identify the woman who torched his house?" asked Goodman.

"Again, no," Lodge said. "He has no sense of having known her, or why she might pick his house to burn down. Sam had moved to town only a couple of months ago, and had no enemies. He is as bewildered as we are.

"I am afraid we will just have to wait until new leads present themselves," Lodge added.

It was not a long wait. One of the police detectives appeared from around the corner. He had been examining trash cans lining a neighboring alley, and had found an empty kerosene can.

"Do you think this has any relevance?" he asked, "or did one of the neighbors just have a big barbeque?"

Lodge took the can, holding it gingerly to preserve fingerprints and other possible evidence. His eyes lit up immediately: he had made an important mental connection.

"Excellent work! This will let me break open the case." He studied the can—or more precisely, the invisible dimensions of the can—for quite a few minutes. We all waited patiently, lest we disturb him.

"This case grows more and more bizarre by the moment," he began. "The woman who murdered Sam lives just a couple of miles from here. She drove here in the middle of the night, doused his house with kerosene, and then set it on fire, killing Sam. Yet she does not have any understanding of why. She is as bewildered as we are—and immersed in guilt and shame as well."

"Does she have a name?" Chief Goodman asked.

"Pamela," Lodge answered.

"If we knew a last name, we might be able to arrest her."

"The last name is unimportant," Lodge added. "She plans to walk into a precinct station in about forty-five minutes and surrender."

"Are you sure?" asked Jack.

Lodge nodded. "Surrendering to you was my idea," he said, "and she leapt at it enthusiastically. She is not a murderer—at least not consciously. She needs to find out what happened last night as much as we do, so that she can understand how she could do something that 'passeth understanding,' as it is stated in the Bible."

"So don't just stand there, Walter!" Jack exhorted. "Tell us what happened!"

"I wish I knew," Lodge said. "But again I am facing a clueless trail."

"Well, I hope you read Pamela her Miranda rights before you told her to turn herself in," chuckled Goodman. "I would hate to lose this case in court over a failure to advise the suspect of her rights telepathically!"

I smelled the faint trace of crabapple, and I knew Lodge had just locked onto the key to the case.

"What did you say?" Lodge asked the chief.

"I made a joke about reading Pamela her Miranda rights."

Lodge stroked his chin. "Miranda, Miranda. There is a connection here. I don't know what it is yet, but there is a connection." He thought a few minutes, and then the gleam of discovery appeared on his face. I knew he had solved the case.

"This is one of the most convoluted cases I have ever encountered. I am sure you will all agree with me, once I have laid out the full story. If I were listening to the story I am about to tell, I am not sure I would even believe it. But it is true. And it illustrates the way the intelligence of life creates opportunities." He took a deep breath and then began.

"Pamela is an identical twin sister of Miranda."

"Miranda?" we all chorused in unison.

"That's right, Miranda," Lodge confirmed. "I would still be clueless if Adam had not made his joke.

"Miranda lives in another city, more than one hundred miles away. She does not see Pamela much any more, but they continue an odd trait of identical twins—they often think or do exactly the same thing at the same moment, even though they are not physically together."

I was beginning to see where Lodge was heading. "You mean it was Miranda who committed the actual crime? Pamela was somehow performing just a shadow enactment of what Miranda was doing a hundred miles away?"

"Something like that," Lodge replied. "Miranda had an argument last night with her boy friend—a person that Pamela does not know. Her boy friend said some pretty nasty things about Miranda, and left her to walk home from the club where they had been dancing. With every mile Miranda had to walk, she got more and more angry at her boy friend. By the time she got home, she was blind with rage. She got in her car, drove to an all night gas station, and bought five gallons of kerosene. She then drove over to her boyfriend's house, doused a shrub by the front porch with kerosene, lit it, stashed the kerosene can in an empty trash can down the alley, and sped off. She went home, quite satisfied with herself, climbed into bed, and fell asleep. The boyfriend's house burned down, and he died in the blaze. She is still sleeping.

"Pamela, waking in the middle of the night, played her part in this strange drama as though she were hypnotized. She was mimicking the acts of her twin sister Miranda, as she had done so many times before."

"But why did she choose Sam?" I asked. "And how do I fit in?"

"You are the best clue of all," Lodge responded. "But we will get to you in a minute. Poor Sam had the misfortune to be an identical twin as well—an identical twin of Miranda's boyfriend. Pamela could not just pick out anyone at random to burn alive—her intense connection to Miranda led her to the very house in our city where the twin brother of

Miranda's boyfriend lay sleeping innocently."

"That's not possible!" said Jack in disbelief.

"I would not have thought so, either," Lodge replied. "But it has happened, so it must be possible." He turned to me. "You knew Miranda's boyfriend in the army. You arrested him once when you were in the military police."

"For what?" I asked.

"For arson," Lodge replied. "He tried to burn down his own barracks."

"Jim Gorman?" I asked. "He's the brother of Sam?"

Lodge nodded yes.

"He carved me up pretty good with a knife when I arrested him."

"Which is why you woke up with such a strong impression. Between the walled-in memory of the chauffeur and your own recollection of Jim, it would have been incredible if you had managed not to have your dream."

"I still don't understand why she went for Jim's brother, rather than her own boy friend," I said.

Lodge's eyes twinkled. "Aaah," he said. "This is where crime becomes mystery. Sam had been Pamela's boyfriend in an earlier life. He had killed her in a fit of rage, when he found her in a passionate embrace in the arms of Jim—that is, the person who was Jim until a few hours ago. Jim, in that earlier lifetime, had been married to the person who we are now calling Miranda. Miranda has been lusting for revenge for thousands of year since.

"As you can see, life does survive death. So, unfortunately, does vengeance. Pamela and Miranda, in and out of incarnation, have been plotting this moment for lifetimes. That is why they incarnated together now as twins. It is also why Sam yielded to an irresistible pull to move to our city just a few months ago. It was the pull of his own untidy karma that brought him here."

Adam whistled. "That surely is a whole new interpretation of Miranda's rights!" He got the laugh he had expected.

"It was a 'right' in the eyes of Miranda, to be sure," Lodge agreed. "But it is not a right that the law can uphold."

As we walked back to the car to drive home, the case having been solved, I asked Lodge one last question: "Why did the intelligence of life allow this scheme of vengeance to proceed?"

"It not only allowed it," Lodge replied, "it actively supported it. Among other things, it caused Jim and Sam to incarnate as identical twins to allow Pamela and Miranda to execute their shameful plot.

"The intelligence of life is a huge system we

are all meant to tap into and rely upon. It is just like my experiments in turning on our lights with my mind. The electrical system in my house will respond regardless of my purpose in having the lights on. Perhaps I am planning to commit a crime. Would you expect the lights to refuse my request because they did not approve of my purpose?"

"No, I guess not."

"It's no different in human life," Lodge pronounced. "It's all in the mind."

Eleven

Gypsies!

"Gypsies!" proclaimed Lodge. We had completed dinner and were lounging in the living room—Lodge called it the parlor—each occupied in his own pursuits.

I looked up from the crossword puzzle I was trying to decipher. "What?"

"Gypsies!" Lodge repeated. "The boy was kidnapped by gypsies."

"Lodge, have you gone over the edge? There aren't any gypsies within a continent of here."

"How wrong you are," crowed Lodge. "There is a band of them operating just a few miles north of here, camped in an RV park outside of town. They arrived only a week ago. I don't expect them to stay long. They prey on a city, then quickly move elsewhere."

"So, what do they have to do with a kidnapped boy? We are not even working on a case of kidnapping. What boy are you talking about?"

"The mayor will be calling us in no more than thirty minutes," Lodge replied, with an air of satisfaction. It would be misleading to describe it as smug, because Lodge is never arrogant or haughty. He is charming and easy going. But he does take pleasure in solving mysteries—even ones that have not yet happened.

"Can you tell me about it now?" I asked.

"To the degree that I understand it, of course. The son of a wealthy merchant has been kidnapped—abducted while walking home from school this afternoon. The kidnappers have contacted the family and are demanding five million dollars for his safe return. The kidnappers, of course, are these gypsies. They are holding the boy in their caravan, which makes him almost impossible to find. Gypsy bands are extended families, and they shield one another from danger. In this case, of course, the whole band is in on the crime together. And it simply is not possible to get a search warrant for thirty to forty RV's.

"The boy is alive—but I have been examining the history of this family of gypsies. They do not have a very good record of returning their hostages unharmed. Most are returned quite dead."

I gulped. The thought was not cheery "The real mystery of this case, therefore," Lodge continued, "is not whodunit or why, but rather: can we recover the boy before they kill him?"

"And how," I muttered, anticipating more physical involvement than normal in this case.

"Exactly, Morgan," Lodge agreed. "And how."

Lodge thought for several minutes without saying a word. He was not thinking as you or I would think, searching randomly for some clue that might illumine us in our confusion. No, he was focusing the powerful search light of his mind on invisible records, histories, patterns, and other sources that might yield a clue as to how best to approach this puzzle. He could research records dating back hundreds of thousands of years in a blink of the inner eye—not historical records, of course, but records inscribed in the intelligent substance of universal life—the Archives, as Lodge usually called them.

"Do you believe in the human soul, Morgan?" Lodge asked me at last.

"I am a good Catholic, Lodge—you know that," I replied.

"Ah, of course. So you believe in the soul, even though you have no idea whatsoever what it is!"

I laughed. "Something like that, I suppose. But I have a hunch that I am going to find out a lot more about the soul than I presently know before the night is out."

"We can hope so," Lodge agreed. "This is a case that will be won or lost at the level of the soul."

"Did they kidnap a boy—or his soul?" I asked.

Lodge looked at me as though I had caught him by surprise. "Keep some of that wit for when company arrives," he said. He turned serious.

"There is some hope for the boy. He was not drawn into this scheme because of any need to pay off past debts or obligations. It is his mother and father—especially the father—who have lessons to learn. Securing the boy's release is going to cost the father dearly, and I am not talking in terms of money. He is going to have to learn to love something other than himself and his personal goals. He will have to learn to communicate his affection and love to his son, or the son will die."

"I'm not sure I fully understand."

Lodge chuckled lightly, almost gently. "I'm struggling with the concept myself. The boy has a rich destiny; his plan for this life is not scheduled to end tonight. But this plan cannot be realized unless the father commits himself to some serious character reform.

"In fact, this kidnapping is a moment of decision for many of the people involved—in fact, everyone except the child. The father must step out of his self-absorption in the superficial rewards of life. The mother must decide to think for herself, and stop being swayed by status. The gypsies need to decide to turn from their murderous ways.

"The final outcome will be determined by the soul of the boy, based on how the other players respond. It must decide whether to continue to live—or withdraw from this lifetime."

"Would the soul actually let its personality be killed?"

Lodge stared straight through me with his piercing eyes. "It happens every day, Morgan. What do you think murder is? The soul of the victim could always stop it, if it wanted to—except in some crimes of passion, perhaps. It chooses not to interfere because the murder serves its purposes for growth and discipline in some way."

"But a little boy?"

"It sounds vicious and cruel, doesn't it?" Lodge agreed. "Well, it isn't. It is actually a demonstration of compassion and care. The soul does not want the boy to become trapped in the materialistic priorities that have imprisoned the character of the father and mother. It would rather withdraw from this life than expose its personality to this kind of conditioning.

"The soul is using the kidnapping as a final effort to force the father to come to grips with his shortcomings. The gypsies are just pawns in a larger drama—which is often the case for most people."

"What horrible things has the father done to precipitate this crisis?" I asked.

"Nothing all that horrible," Lodge replied. "He is primarily guilty of sins of omission, more than comission. He has neglected his son and his wife. He provides them with an elegant lifestyle, but ignores their human needs. He is letting himself be lured into an affair which would destroy his marriage. The problem is that the son's future depends heavily on interacting with his father. The father has the capacity to nurture his child just by spending time with him. There are certain intangible qualities in his character that will rub off and be picked up by the lad if only they spend enough time together—and this is exactly what the lad needs. The boy's soul sees all of this slipping away, and has taken dramatic action to change the course of events."

"Does this kind of thing happen often?" I

asked. "I mean the soul taking action to change established trends of events?"

"Absolutely," said Lodge. "But we seldom have any inkling of it. It all happens behind the scenes, as it were. And it is only rarely that the soul must endanger the personality in this way in order to straighten out its life's destiny."

It was at this stage in our discussion that the mayor arrived, with the father and mother in tow. Lodge and I shifted from the living room to Walter's office to receive them. The mother was hysterical; the father was angry and irritated, blaming Jack for "not keeping the streets safe for young children walking home from school."

Jack introduced the parents—John and Elsie Wexford—first to Lodge and then to me. He identified Lodge as a "thought detective," the term Lodge prefers. This incited Wexford even more. "Why are you wasting our time consulting a psychic?" he demanded. "I am a realist, a business man. I do not appreciate being mocked in this way while my only son is in the hands of kidnappers—perhaps murderers!"

I generally keep my peace in these kinds of situations. But it suddenly occurred to me that Lodge had been filling me in with the arcane details of the case for a reason. Almost as if I had digested an insight in one swallow, I knew that Lodge wanted me to speak.

There was also the faint fragrance of crabapple—not in the room, but in my mind. I was not sure how that could be possible, but it was a time for action, not reflection.

I handed Lodge a twenty dollar bill. "You win, Lodge," I said. "He is everything you said he would be—and more. I'm not sure he deserves to get his boy back."

Lodge accepted the money, silently congratulating me on the unexpected addition of a manufactured wager. The wife began bellowing all over again. Jack looked stunned, never having seen this from us before. Wexford blew up.

"This is outrageous! My boy is in the hand of criminals, and you stand there insulting me!"

"Oh, I wasn't insulting you," I responded. "If anything, it was you who insulted Walter, by making demeaning remarks about his mental skills before you even got to know him. It is typical of people like you, who think they know all the answers, but are not even willing to look under a few rocks for the obvious ones. So, I thought I would introduce you to Walter Lodge's skills and abilities.

"In the twenty minutes before you arrived, without any advance notice of your appearance, Walter has been telling me all about you. He told me that you are self-centered, egotistical, and driven by your own earlier failures. He told me that you spend no time at home, and almost completely ignore your wife and her needs. From what I learned, you are the kind of man who equates money with everything. You seem to believe that money can substitute for love, it can substitute for companionship, it can substitute for happiness—it can substitute for everything! How did you even know your son was missing? You are never around!"

I could scarcely believe my ears. The words just tumbled out of my mouth, as though I actually knew what I was saying. At one dimension of my being, I knew that everything I said was true. But in my conscious self, I was caught completely by surprise. So was everyone else.

Mrs. Wexford stopped blubbering and began listening. "How do you know all this? It is absolutely true! John is never at home; he is always consumed with a driving passion to make more money."

"I am just repeating what Lodge told me, when he first became aware—through mental detection—that your son had been kidnapped."

"Th-this kind of thing cannot be done," said Wexford.

"In your world, that is true," I replied. "But you are no longer in your world. You must step into our world, if you want your son returned. It will be a big leap, but you must make it."

Wexford sat down, his head in his hands. "This is all so confusing. I want my son back. I will pay anything. Anything."

Lodge re-entered the fray. "That is the problem, Mr. Wexford. You cannot re-purchase your son for any amount of money. Once you pay, he will be returned to you—but dead."

Elsie Wexford began bellowing again; John Wexford looked like he had seen his own ghost.

"That is their modus operandi," Lodge continued. "You are in a vicious trap. Even I cannot guarantee the safe return of your son. But I can assure you that paying the ransom is the equivalent of signing his death warrant.

"By the way, how much ransom are the kidnappers demanding?"

Wexford looked at the mayor, reluctant to give out vital information.

"My impression was five million dollars," said Lodge coolly.

"To the penny," Jack confirmed. "You never cease to amaze me, Lodge."

"What else do you know about this affair that you haven't told us?" Wexford inquired. "And how do you know it? The kidnapping just happened this afternoon. It has not been reported in the press. Jack is the only one other than Elsie and I who know about it. How can you know all of these details? Are you in on the plot?"

Jack blanched, Elsie choked, I fidgeted, and Lodge laughed. "I expected you to say that sooner or later. It is the typical conclusion of a thinminded thinker."

"A thinminded thinker? What's that?" asked Elsie.

"Someone who thinks there is only one answer to any question. Someone like your husband, who thinks that money is always the answer to every question."

"It's worked for me so far," Wexford replied.

"It may have seemed to," Lodge corrected gently. "But in fact, it has not. You cannot buy your wife and pay for her in installments, like you are paying for that rock she's wearing on her finger. You cannot buy a son. You cannot buy a reputation in the community. You have to earn these things through more subtle coin—respect, trust, affection, and love."

He paused a moment. "How and when have you been directed to pay it?"

"We have been given twenty-four hours. I am to place a briefcase with cash on the Fourth Street bridge, and drive away. They will pick it up, count it, then release my son where they picked him up. If they are watched or followed, he dies."

"The usual approach of the police would be to deliver the ransom," Jack chipped in, "then try to arrest them when they dropped off the boy."

"Which is precisely why they will kill the child once they have gotten the money, and make no attempt to deliver him anywhere. They will disappear into thin air, untraceable."

"How do you know?" asked Wexford.

"I have studied their methods mentally. They are a band of gypsies. They do not live here in the city. They don't live anywhere, really. They will scatter to the ends of the globe, then regroup in a few months and perpetrate the same crime in a completely different locale."

Lodge turned to Jack. "Have the police check their computer for unsolved kidnappings. You will find at least six that fit this description over the last three or four years—each one of them hundreds of miles from the others. So far, police have not made the link."

"Well, what are we to do?" asked Elsie Wexford.

"Plan on delivering the money as demanded," said Lodge. "And then go to confession."

"What?" hollered John Wexford. "What kind of weak-kneed, feeble response is that? You just said yourself that paying the ransom would sign his death warrant."

"I will admit to warning you that paying the ransom alone would be the same as killing your son," Lodge agreed, "but I do not recall putting any such limitation on the power of confession. It takes a lot more strength than you can imagine to get down on your knees and confess. It also generates a whole lot more power. It's too bad you are not Catholic—you might understand."

Wexford was experiencing difficulty putting his "people skills" to work. "Okay, so tell me—how does confessing save the life of my child?"

"The kidnappers are a band of gypsies. Most of them still speak only Romany, the language of gypsies. They came to this country years ago from Europe. How they got to Europe is a mystery to historians, but it is something I investigated tonight, while waiting for you to arrive. Gypsies were originally inhabitants of India, one of the lower castes. They rebelled against the caste system, only to be persecuted for their rebellion—and exiled. So they left India and became nomads, wandering through the general region of Persia. Eventually, their travels took them to Europe, where they were mistaken for 'Egyptians'—and called 'gypsies.' They have developed intense family ties and a very anti-social attitude. It means nothing to them to kidnap and even murder non-gypsies.

"But they are also very superstitious. They can be persuaded not to kill your child quite easily—but not by any action you, the police, or I could possibly hope to take.

"This must be left to divine intervention. I have researched this in great detail. The child's soul wants your son to live—it has a rich and productive future planned for him. But if you continue to ignore your son as you have been doing, he will grow up a spoiled brat, unable to harness his inner potential. The soul shrinks at horror from that prospect, and would rather let the gypsies kill the boy than have him grow up and be trapped in the excesses of your lifestyle.

"You must convince the soul that you have seen the error of your lifestyle and are willing to change. The only way I know that you can do that in the next twenty-four hours is through confession—a full, complete confession in which you repent the ways of the past, atone for them, and accept your own soul's higher guidance for the future."

"But how do I do this? As you said, I am not Catholic."

"I am not Catholic, either," Lodge said. "Neither am I a priest. But I bring certain powers with me from earlier lives. I have the authority to hear your confession—and to ascertain if it is heartfelt. Nothing less will suffice."

"This is sounding more and more hokey by the minute," Wexford said gruffly. "But under the circumstances, I am willing to grasp at straws. How do we proceed?"

"Follow me," Lodge directed. He rose and motioned Wexford toward the door. The two of them went off to a private room, leaving Jack, Elsie Wexford, and me.

"How long will they be gone?" Elsie asked.

"I have no idea. But if Lodge can figure out a way to return your son to you, he'll do it," I said, adding: "He's the only man that has a chance of saving the life of your boy."

Jack nodded in agreement.

We talked in this way for quite a while, giving Elsie as much hope as we dared impart, knowing the uncertainty of the outcome. After an hour or so, I thought to call out for pizzas.

"It's going to be a long night," I remarked. "No reason why we should go hungry."

It was another forty-five minutes before the pizza arrived. I heard the delivery car pull up; it tripped an alarm embedded in the driveway which had been installed by the original occupant of the house, a man Lodge called The Gentleman.

I went to the door to accept the pizza, but was confronted by a different sight instead. Another car had pulled up behind the pizza delivery, and three thugs had gotten out and were in the process of robbing the delivery boy of his money—and our pizza! I instantly thought of Lodge and crabapple, knowing my thought would be enough to alert him to this sudden development. Then I grabbed my revolver, which I always left hanging in its holster in the hall closet, and ran out to confront the thugs.

In this case, I had both intelligence and the element of surprise on my side—and perhaps hunger as well. I shot out the tires of their car and the delivery van, so that no one could attempt an escape. I yelled to the pizza boy to hit the ground. I then fired a couple of warning shots at the thugs and told them to toss down their guns. They looked at each other in surprise and confusion, and dropped their guns before realizing that it was they who had the advantage.

I smelled the faint aroma of crabapple once again, and knew that Lodge had helped out, instilling a second or two of confusion in the minds of the three robbers at the critical moment. I yelled to Jack to come help me; he and the pizza boy handcuffed the three of them as quickly as they could. I know there had been two handcuffs in a chest of drawers in the hall, but where the third pair came from, I do not know. We herded the thugs into the kitchen, where Lodge, Wexford, his wife, and Jack were waiting.

The pizza boy stood in the kitchen with a look of shock on his face.

"I'll call your boss and tell him you are being detained as part of an investigation into a crime ring that you helped us break up," said Jack to the pizza man. "In the meantime, sit down and have some of the pizza. This must have been one of your roughest deliveries."

"It all depends on how much of a tip I get," said the pizza lad, trying to sound as if all of his deliveries ended this way, "and if I have to pay for four new tires."

In the bright light of the kitchen, we got our first good look at the thiefs. They were as young as the pizza boy, in their late teens, with dark, swarthy skin and the look of trapped foxes.

"They look like street urchins from the alleys of Calcutta," Elsie Wexford said, almost compassionately. I thought she was going to offer them some of the pizza, but she held back.

Lodge examined them thoughtfully and turned to Wexford. "I think you can start breathing more easily. Your confession was sincere."

"How do you know that?" asked Elsie, suddenly more curious than afraid. It was as though she sensed that everything was going to turn out all right—and these thieves were the reason why.

"These three thugs are part of the gypsy family that kidnapped your son. They wanted to go on a lark tonight, and ended up deciding to rob a pizza delivery car—just for the fun of it. They could have picked any pizza truck in town—there must be hundreds out on a night like tonight. But they happened to pick this one, delivering pizzas ordered by Morgan, to the very address where you and your wife had come seeking help from me. I generally view such impossible coincidences as signs from higher intelligence that our requests are being answered."

Lodge turned to the three and said something in a tongue I could not comprehend. They answered in the same strange language. Lodge replied, and their faces went pale. They started jabbering among themselves, crossing themselves as though they had just confronted Satan himself.

Lodge turned back to the rest of us. "I just informed them that I knew who they were, and I knew their family. I told them that they had made a terrible mistake this afternoon, kidnapping a boy who was protected under the blessing of the Virgin Mary. I further informed them that they had one hour to appeal to the rest of the family to bring back the boy unharmed and to turn themselves in to the authorities, or they each would die a pitiful and painful death, involving much retching."

"Are you able to make such bold statements?"

"I *have* the authority to make such statements, but I wasn't actually *using* it. I was just playing on their superstitious minds. The fact that they were lured here and then captured is enough to make them believe anything I say at the moment."

He was interrupted by one of the three asking him, in the strange language, to use the telephone. He called a number, then started talking like a machine gun to someone at the other end. He paused, apparently waiting for the person answering the telephone to pass it on—it must have been a cell phone—to the chief gypsy in the band. Then he started rattling away again, in rapid fire. He abruptly hung up, then sat down, looking very depressed.

Lodge turned to the Wexfords. "I think Morgan acted with unusual foresight tonight, when he ordered these pizzas. Your son will be delivered here in about fifteen minutes, safe and unharmed."

He then turned to Jack. "The gypsy family will turn themselves in at the same time, so you better have Chief Goodman send over several police vans to take them down to the station. They are willing to plead guilty to the charge of attempted kidnapping if other charges are dropped. You ought to be able to put them away for the rest of their lives."

Hours later, when everyone had left, I wearily asked Lodge: "How did you create such a rapid transformation in Wexford?"

Lodge smiled faintly. "I don't think I had much to do with it. He was ready to change, or he would not have been able to do it. I just had to break through the outer layer of resistance—the thick shell of habit that had built up like a layer of dust on a piece of furniture.

"It wasn't easy, and for the first hour, I was despairing of our chances. He was willing to confess, but only as a pro forma gesture. He had learned all too well how to dissemble sincerity while not meaning it. The confession, in short, was not working. It was not drawing any response from his spirit.

"Finally, I told him to stop. He looked at me in a funny way, and that one moment of hesitation and doubt on his part was all I needed. I projected into his thoughts the image of his son lying dead on their front yard. I then let him see the impact on his wife the lad's death would have, and how such an outcome would affect his life.

"It was a rather frightening prospect, and it woke him up. He began to reach out genuinely for help. He opened his heart to the love of the soul, and his soul embraced him and renewed him. I did not have to do anything more. He did the rest.

"Didn't you think he had passed the test when you saw him embrace his son, running up to the door?" Lodge asked.

"Frankly," I said, "I could only think of one

thing. Here was a man who had been walking around with two people inside him. One man was insecure, materialistic, and self-absorbed; the other was kind, gentle, and full of loving strength. I guess the immature person had beaten up and gagged the mature person, until a crisis came along to free the better man."

"Well put, Morgan!" Lodge said. "And I think we may have gained some new friends in the process. The new John Wexford is certainly a man worth knowing.

"And none of this could have happened without the gypsies."

And then he said something I could not understand in the strange tongue he had used in speaking with the gypsies. I stared at him quizzically and he laughed.

"It's all in the mind," he roared. "It's all in the mind!"

Twelve

Murder by Proxy

Lodge was in one of his Thespian moods, reading excerpts from some ancient play in a voice strong enough to wake the dead. " *'Qué es la vida? Un frenesí. Qué es la vida? Una illusión, una sombra, una ficción.'* " He lay down his book and stared at me. "Ah, but I forget. You don't know Spanish. The hero of the story, a prince, has been imprisoned in a tower by his father since birth, because the king misread omens suggesting he would be killed by his son. And the hero asks: 'What is life? A fit of madness. What is life? An illusion, a shadow, a story.' It is a great philosophical portrait of life, don't you think? *'La vida es sueño.'* Life is only a dream—until we awaken."

"I don't know," I replied. "Last night I dreamed I was shot by a bullet, but this morning I find myself healthy and whole. Ordinarily I think of bullets as quite real, but last night's bullet must have been an illusion. So, if life is a dream, it must also be unreal."

"Not unreal," Lodge corrected, enjoying the banter, "just something you imagined. We tend to define real and unreal as visible and invisible. But that definition does not work. Oxygen is invisible, but quite definitely real. The better definition of reality is what we know. If we know something second hand, by hearing about it or reading about it, we do not know if it is real. If we imagine something, we do not know if it is real—in fact, the odds are that it is not. But if we have thought about something to the extent of penetrating to the core of its existence, then we know from what roots it sprung—and if it is real or not."

I was not sure I understood anything of what he had just said. "So, how does that apply to last night's bullet?"

"If you had traced it back to its source, you would have found that it came not from a gun but from your own subconscious fears. You periodically have dreams about being shot, even though this is the first time you have bothered to tell me about one. This was just another one of those anxiety dreams."

"Are you sure it is not a prophetic dream?" I asked.

Lodge laughed. "Absolutely. Besides, our next case is going to involve poison, not guns."

That woke me up with a bang. "Next case?" I asked.

Lodge sneaked a peak out of the window.

"I believe Jack is walking up to the house even now," he said.

It was indeed his honor the mayor, our friend Jack Steele.

"Come in and join us for a cup of coffee on this fine morning," bellowed Lodge cheerily as we entered the kitchen. Jack found an empty chair at the table, while our housekeeper, Mrs. Milledge, poured him a steaming cup of coffee.

"What brings you to my threshold?" Lodge asked jovially.

"I had a dream last night," Jack began.

"It's contagious!" Lodge exclaimed. "We've just been talking about dreams. Can you tell what is a dream and what is reality?"

"If I could," Jack replied. "I wouldn't be here consulting with you."

We could see Jack was distressed by something, so we eased off the joviality. "Tell us about it," I suggested, offering Jack some sweet rolls.

"Malcolm Bright, a prominent lawyer in town, died a week ago while he was sleeping. His body was found in the morning by his wife. She called the police and asked what to do; they suggested calling a funeral home. They picked up the body, she had it cremated, and then conducted a lovely memorial service.

I knew Bright professionally, so I attended the service.

"This morning, I woke up in a fright, with a vivid image of Malcom appearing right before me, repeating the single word: 'Murder.' It scared the daylights out of me, I can tell you." Jack was still shaking as he related his experience to us.

I turned to Lodge. "Well, Walter—is the bullet real, or just a dream?"

Walter thought for a few moments, scanning the inner reaches of Jack's mind, in search of one rather frightening dream experience.

"This dream is not just a dream," he said at last. "It is a very real message from beyond." He turned to Jack, his patented playfulness dancing in his eyes.

"Congratulations, Your Honor. You have just managed to raise the dead. It should help you immensely during your next campaign for office."

"That's not much comfort, when you put it that way," Jack retorted. "But now the issue is: what do we do? I can't very well reopen the case on the strength of a one-word dream. I can't even order the body exhumed, to find out how he was killed. It's nothing but ashes."

"Oh, we know how he was killed," I volunteered. "He was poisoned."

Jack turned and stared at me. "And how do you know this?"

"Walter was telling me all about it as you walked up the lane."

"I merely said that our next case would involve poisoning. Then you showed up."

"Well, it's as good a place to start as any, but our problem remains. How do we prove it? And what do we prove? There is no body to examine."

"In a case like this," Lodge suggested, "there is only one thing we can do. Ask the victim."

"Ask the victim?" replied Jack. "How? He's dead."

"He spoke to you last night, didn't he?" Lodge replied. "It would be unsociable not to speak to you again—but this time through me. I will leave it to the two of you to ask the right questions."

With that, he leaned back in his chair, closed his eyes, and stepped out of his body. A few moments passed, and he seemed to step back into his body. But it wasn't Lodge returning. It was someone entirely new.

It took several minutes before he was comfortable and could speak. "I asked what I was supposed to say," he began, "and the chap I passed leaving as I was arriving suggested, 'Good morning.' So, *good morning!*"

It was a strong, dominating personality—but clearly not Lodge. The essence of Lodge was nowhere to be found. An entirely different personage was sitting there, operating Lodge's body and subconscious as though it were a puppet show.

Jack was too stunned to respond. So I took over. I had been a part of numerous Lodge seances; it was old hat to me. "And a good morning to you, sir. Could you tell us your name?"

"Until a week ago, I was known as Malcolm Bright. Since I died, I have discovered that I have had other names, too—names I had before I became Malcolm Bright."

"Do you know how you died?" I asked. "It is assumed here that you died naturally, in your sleep."

"No," Malcolm replied. "I was poisoned. Arsenic. Small doses over a span of three months—until I died."

"Do you know who poisoned you?"

"Yes," Malcolm replied, in nothing more than a whisper. "My wife."

"Are you sure?"

"I would never cast even a shadow of suspicion on my wife unless I was absolutely sure."

"Well, how can you be so sure?"

"Several weeks before I died, I saw her mixing a powder into my drink—a sight I was not supposed to see. Later, I procured the vial and had it examined. It was lined with a thin film of arsenic. That is when I knew why my health had been gradually failing."

"Did you confront her?"

"No."

"Did you try to stop her?"

"No."

"Did you inform anyone about it?"

"No."

"Well, why not, man?"

"It may seem odd to you, but I dearly loved my wife. We had been married for almost twenty years, and I adored her. I could not believe that she was trying to kill me. But then a worse thought occurred to me. She obviously no longer loved me! She was trying to kill me, for God's sake. And I realized I might as well let her finish the deed. I would not want to live anyway if I had her arrested and convicted of trying to murder me. I could not live with a broken heart. So I just let her finish the job."

"Why did you come to me this morning and tell me it was murder, then?" asked Jack.

"After I died, I found I was trapped. By not reporting what I had learned to the police, I had actually strengthened my attachment to my wife. I had died for love. But in this past week, I have come to realize that it was not love—it was just an attachment. I loved the person I thought was my wife, but I obviously did not know her very well.

"My understanding of love began to weaken as I made these discoveries. Then, I was informed that until I broke my attachment to her, I would not be able to move on in the after life. I would become a ghost, desperately haunting her, seeking release. Still I resisted, reluctant, I guess, to give up something I had died for—foolishly, as it turns out. Then I saw the wisdom of the advice. I had no desire to become a poster child for unrequited love.

"So, this is my act of detachment. Thank you for letting me have this opportunity."

Having said that, he melted away pretty much as he had appeared. A minute or two passed, and Lodge suddenly, forcefully stepped back into his body. "Well, that was refreshing! I ought to step out of my body more regularly after breakfast. Have I mentioned how charming the Tivoli gardens are at this time of day?"

He paused, then asked Mrs. Milledge, who had been quietly observing the seance from the kitchen: "Molly, may I have another cup of coffee, please—just to remind me of where I am?"

Jack was still not satisfied. "Okay. I am convinced that Malcolm was murdered by his wife. But we have no proof, no evidence to build a case on. Where do we go from here?"

Lodge agreed. "Where, indeed? We have a very interesting moral case here. We know that Mrs. Bright set out to murder her husband, who subsequently died as a result of her actions. It looks like murder—but is it? Malcolm discovered her plot a few weeks before he died. He had ample opportunity to turn her in, or at least sequester himself in a hospital, where he could have been treated. But he chose not to do so. Is it still murder—or does it now become suicide?"

"It cannot be suicide," I interjected, "because he did nothing to set these acts in motion. He simply accepted the death penalty of a higher court—namely the court of love, his love for his wife. She still murdered him, I say. And she certainly believes she did. She was oblivious to the fact that he did not resist her efforts to murder him—plus, she made sure she covered her tracks by having him cremated."

"An excellent analysis, Morgan," Lodge said. "I am inclined to go with that interpretation myself. Malcolm confirmed the murder, but he was not exactly forthright in everything he said. Even ghosts can dissemble, you know. He is still very much in love with his wife, and is trying to protect her, even though he knows he must detach from her.

"While I was out of my body, letting Malcolm hold forth, I used my nose to sniff around a bit. Among other things, I intuitively examined the contents of the subconscious of Mrs. Evelyn Bright.

"It seems that Evelyn was as thoroughly devoted to her husband as Malcom was to her. She was highly protective of her husband, and very attentive to his needs. She would have been the last person I would have expected to murder a spouse, at least based on a superficial reading of her character. There were seeds of murder planted deep in her character, but so deep that they never crept into her conscious awareness on their own. They had to be excavated and watered.

"Three years ago, as a gesture of his deep love for his wife, Malcolm bought a term life insurance policy on himself, insuring himself for three million dollars. Naturally, he named Evelyn as his beneficiary. When he told his wife what he had done, she was overwhelmed by the magnitude of this gesture; if anything ever happened to Malcolm, she would be able to live without any worries about money. She was thrilled, to say the least.

"About six months later, however, those seeds deep in her unconscious mind began to stir. She was minding her own business, knitting a sweater for Malcolm, when a voice in her head proposed sticking one of her knitting needles into Malcolm's heart, in order to get the three million dollars. She was horrified that she would ever entertain such a thought, dropped her knitting, and went over to the bar, where she poured herself a Scotch, downing it in one gulp. It was a preposterous notion, and she rejected it. But she made the fatal mistake of assuming that it was her own thought.

"Over the next two years, the thoughts arose again and again, at large intervals of time at first, and then more frequently. She fought valiantly to resist the powerful temptation at first, but then began to give in, as though she was being seduced into having an affair. The murderous courtship lasted until six months ago, when she began to succumb. The night she sealed her fate—and Malcolm's—was the night she stopped fighting the voices of temptation and began planning how she might murder her husband. She had embarked on a downward spiral from which there was no retreat.

"You want evidence? The insurance policy itself is evidence. In fact, if there is any suspicion of foul play at all, the insurance company will be more than willing to conduct its own investigation. Even if there is not enough evidence to convict her of murder, there certainly will be enough evidence to deny her the insurance payout—and perhaps charge her with insurance fraud."

"Meaning?"

"Evelyn concocted the plan to poison her husband with repeated low doses of arsenic because he was twenty years her senior—a man already in his sixties—and it would be plausible for him to become sickly and die. In fact, people would be sure to note that he was starting to look feeble, as the arsenic took hold. She also knew that their friends often commented on how hard Malcolm worked—saying, in essence, that he was killing himself. It would be perfectly normal if he started to fail.

"So far so good. But being inexperienced in the fine art of murder—as she was in this lifetime—she made a classic mistake. She went to a pharmacy in Bridgepath, about thirty miles from here, to make her purchases. She did this because she did not want to be recognized. But she forgot that in a town the size of Bridgepath, the pharmacist knows every one of his regular customers by name. She was memorable precisely because she was unknown. She was also memorable because she is a stunning example of womanhood—and was dressed more for a visit to the theater than to make a quick run to the pharmacy. The pharmacist can confirm that she bought arsenic on several occasions in a three or four month period, for the stated reason of 'killing rats.'

"The insurance detectives will find the empty vials, and traces of arsenic on the bartop counter, where she prepared her deadly drinks." Lodge turned to Jack. "Will that be enough evidence to turn your dream into a turn in prison for Evelyn?"

"I would think so," Jack said.

"Yes, I imagine it would be," Lodge agreed. "And yet, it was not actually Evelyn who killed her husband."

We all looked at Lodge with stunned surprise. "What?"

"The true murderer is another lawyer here in town," Lodge said off-handedly, as though we should have foreseen this possibility from the very beginning, "even though he did not know Evelyn or ever step foot in the Bright house."

"Explain yourself," Jack demanded.

"Of course," said Lodge with a glint of triumph in his eye. "I have not been able to determine his name—lawyers are very skillful at hiding information, even at intuitive levels. But it should become obvious who I am describing as your men begin to examine Malcolm's files.

"This particular lawyer represents the estate of a wealthy industrialist. It is a complicated estate, with numerous trusts, philanthropic bequests, and residual beneficiaries. It was probated twenty years ago, but the trusts run for another ten years. During these twenty years, the lawyer has skimmed about one million dollars from the estate and its trusts, over and above the money he was rightly entitled to be paid.

"Malcolm became involved in a suit against the estate about four years ago, and ever since, the lawyer in question has been living in fear that Malcolm would uncover his embezzlements. This fear—and a certain amount of jealousy regarding Malcolm's greater skill as a lawyer—activated deep-seated patterns of hate and anger in the lawyer's unconscious mind. About three years ago, this became focused toward Malcolm as a permanent 'intent to kill.'

"Now, mind you, the lawyer in question was never consciously aware of this intent to kill.

He dealt with Malcolm on a friendly, professional basis. He was genuinely shocked when he heard of Malcolm's death. It was only hours later that he realized that a major threat to him had been removed. But he did not consciously even take delight in the realization.

"Nonetheless, this 'intent to kill' was like a battering ram that tried to break down Malcolm's defenses twenty-four hours a day. Malcolm was a strong man, however, and gave no openings for the assault to score any serious damage. Malcolm occasionally experienced an unexplained crippling headache, but seldom anything more serious than that.

"This emotional battering ram was already at work, however, when Evelyn began speculating on the insurance policy. The seeds of murder already implanted deep in her unconscious mind—the residue of an earlier life in which she had disposed of five husbands in a row!—were stimulated and awakened by the incessant hammering of the lawyer's projected intent to kill Malcolm. Gradually, the idea of murder took form in Evelyn's unguarded mind, and she signed on as the active agent who would materialize the impulse.

"Evelyn is guilty of complicity to commit murder, but she is not the real murderer. She simply carried out the directed intention of

Malcolm's colleague at the bar. Find him, and you find the real murderer of Malcolm Bright,"

"That's amazing," said Jack. "But I do not see how we can arraign the lawyer, even if we do figure out who he is, for murder. As you would say, 'It's all in the mind.' "

"You're right," Lodge agreed. "But you can nail him for embezzlement from his client. As for Evelyn, it's about time she paid the price for murdering her five husbands two thousand years ago."

We all whistled in amazement.

"The irony," Lodge added, "is that Malcolm seems to have won his last case—by dying. By taking the arsenic, he insured that his colleague's desperate scheme would be exposed—and justice would be served, not once but twice."

Thirteen

A Lot at Stake

Lodge was passing through the parlor, looking thoroughly occupied, even though we were both killing time, with nothing to do. Breakfast had passed uneventfully; we had managed to extend it a half an hour by discussing current political fiascos over coffee. I then retired to the parlor and plunged into a crossword puzzle. Lodge pretended to have something to do, but kept walking through the parlor every ten minutes, hoping something would happen spontaneously.

"While you are here, Walter," I said, "why not help me out? What is a seven-letter word that answers the clue: 'Twenty-two Donalds make up one.' I think the sixth letter is 'u.' "

Lodge did not even have to catch his breath. "Try 'arcanum.' "

"Arcanum? Why?"

"Who do you suppose the Donald is?"

"Trump, I guess."

"Exactly. And twenty-two trumps make what?"

"I don't know," I admitted.

"Oh, come now," Lodge chided me. "Don't tell me that you have never had your fortune read! Thirty-five years old and never been scammed! Imagine!"

I frowned in disapproval of his rebuke. "I didn't say I hadn't been scammed—I was in the military, after all. But I do admit to a complete void in knowledge about fortune telling."

"The reference is to the Tarot—an ancient system of divination involving seventy-eight cards, very much like playing cards," Lodge explained. "In fact, the Tarot is the forerunner of modern playing cards. There are four suits of fourteen cards each, which makes what they call the Minor Arcana. There are also twenty-two other cards, each one an arcanum, which constitutes the Major Arcana. If one Donald makes a Trump, then twenty-two Donalds—or Trumps—must make an arcanum. Where's the mystery in that?"

The moment he uttered the word "mystery," Lodge cocked his head ever so slightly, as was his custom when he became aware of inspiration or intuitive guidance. The faint scent of crabapple filled the room briefly, then dissipated quickly. Something was in the air.

"Do we have any cases on tap?" he asked me abruptly. He knew very well that the answer was no, but I played along with his game.

"Let me check," I said, and very deliberately consulted our appointment book. "Nothing listed here," I said, after skimming the blank pages for about a minute.

"Splendid!" Lodge said. "Then today makes a perfect day to further your education."

"I beg your pardon?"

"We shall visit a gypsy and have the future read with the Tarot," Lodge amplified.

"I'm not sure I want my fortune told," I replied, hesitating, "and if I did, I would rather it came from you."

"That's highly flattering, Morgan," Lodge replied, "but misses the point. We will go to a fortune teller and ask her to tell the future, but you have nothing to worry about. I can assure you she will not be right. These fortune tellers are interested only in one thing: finding a way to separate you from your money. It's a scam, that's all."

"This sounds more and more thrilling by the minute," I replied drily.

"Oh, don't worry about the money. This one's on me."

So we left the house and drove to the commercial establishment of one Madame Flora, who "sees all, knows all, and tells all," according to the lettering on the window pane. Inside, the space had been divided into two small rooms. One was a waiting room with two or three chairs and some signs on the wall. Curses, blessings, and healings were all offered for fixed prices—very reasonable prices, in fact. But in each instance, the price was accompanied by an asterisk. Near the bottom of the sign, the explanation of the asterisk stated that extra charges would apply in "special cases." I am not especially intuitive, but even I could figure out that every case would end up being a "special case."

We were the only ones in the waiting room, a space that had been lavishly decorated in whore house scarlet. Lodge assured me that as fortune tellers go, red velvet is a sign of high esteem and prosperity.

We rang the bell, as a sign instructed us to do. Nothing happened, so we sat down to wait. After about five minutes, we heard someone approaching from the direction of the consulting room. Madame Flora suddenly appeared in the doorway. She was a middle-aged woman, a bit overweight, and was wearing an excessive amount of make-up.

"Good morning," she said cheerily, in a voice that sounded more like it came from the less prosperous districts of Memphis than a gypsy caravan. "May I help you?"

"My friend would like a consultation,"

Lodge said quickly, correctly concerned that if he left the discussion to me, I would say that we were travelling to Albuquerque and had lost our way; could she please give us directions? That, in any event, had been my plan.

"Tarot consultations are $10 apiece," Madame Flora announced.

Lodge handed her the money. "Step this way, gentlemen," she said.

We followed her into her inner sanctum, a simple room with a single round table covered by a splattered tablecloth. Pictures of Jesus and the Buddha hung on the wall. I imagined that both of them were frowning. I had an urge to turn the pictures toward the wall, so they would not have to witness my upcoming humiliation, but I resisted it. A candle was burning as the centerpiece of the table.

We sat down. Madame Flora picked up a Tarot deck that had been laying on the table, thumbed through it, then placed the page of pentacles on the tablecloth, saying that it represented me. It was a large, oversized card, ornately decorated in shabby artwork. The page was dressed in ochre tights under a light green tunic. He had an odd red headdress that draped down over his shoulders. He was holding an orange disc—the pentacle—and seemed to me to be contemplating the infinite opportunities in the world for finding his fortune. I decided this was a sign that I should be out making my fortune, rather than having it told to me! But Lodge's voice filled my mind, even though he said nothing aloud. "In earlier decks, the page of pentacles represented the duality of action and inaction. We are inactive at the time, so she picked this card to represent you. Even she is wondering why she picked it."

At that point, I began to wonder just how spontaneous this visit to the fortune teller had been.

She then placed another card on top of the page, completely covering it. The card was the High Priestess, a woman in mystic garb studying an ancient scroll. She was flanked by two pillars, one black and one white. Between them was a florid tapestry that obscured the longer view. At her feet was a crescent moon. Madame Flora gave no explanation, but placed a second card crosswise on top of the first. The card was Death. Madame Flora hiccupped slightly, but managed to stifle most of her surprise. She quickly dealt the other eight cards:

The five of rods was placed above the other two. It looked like a gang of four thugs pummeling the page with long wooden poles. I shuddered.

The Hermit was placed below the first two. It showed an old man in grey garb looking for something with a lantern on a dark and snowy night. He held a staff in one hand.

The Tower—a castle tower struck by lightning, ablaze with fire, with people falling from the parapets—was placed to the left of the first two cards.

The eight of swords was placed to their right. A woman was tied, blindfolded, and imprisoned by eight vertical swords.

Then Madame Flora started a new column of cards, just to the right of the others: Justice was the first card, on the bottom. It resembled the High Priestess, except in the personage of Justice, who held a sword upright in one hand and the scales of justice in the other.

The Magician was the second card, just above it. He held a wand upright in his hand with the same authority as the Justice.

Judgment was next: an eerie card re-enacting Judgment Day, with an angel calling the dead to rise out of their coffins.

The final card, at the top of the column, was the ten of swords. A man lay face down on the desert floor with ten swords piercing his spine.

The fortune teller glanced at the cards briefly, then turned to me.

"You are in grave danger, my son," she began. "Your own life may be at stake if you do not act quickly."

"What must I do?" I asked.

"You must believe in the power of the Tarot to help you," she replied.

"And what can it do?"

"If you believe, I can cast a spell that will bless you and protect you from the mortal danger you face."

"How do I demonstrate that I believe?"

"By paying as much as you can for the spell."

"How much do you recommend?"

"I cannot say," she replied. "How much can you pay?"

"I could pay fifty bucks," I answered.

"Fifty dollars? This is your life you are fighting for, my son."

"Well, I suppose I could pay one hundred."

Madame Flora looked very unhappy, but decided not to push too far too fast.

"All right, here is what you should do. Come here every morning for the next week. Bring me the one hundred dollars each day, and I will cast the protective spell."

"One hundred dollars every day?" I nearly exploded, but remembered that Lodge was there to keep me out of serious harm. "Why every day?"

"The spell only lasts for one diurnal cycle," said Madame Flora. "It must be renewed every morning." She paused. "Do you have one hundred dollars with you?"

I nodded yes.

"Good. We should do the first spell today, lest the tragedy foreseen in these cards befall you this afternoon."

Lodge broke into the conversation for the first time since the reading began. "What kind of tragedy do you foresee for my friend?"

She seemed to fixate on the final card, the ten of swords. "A business deal has failed, and someone is very disappointed—actually, he is enraged. He will try to exact retribution by killing you."

"I am not involved in any such deal!" I protested indignantly, half rising from my chair. "I work for my friend here. I protect him."

The fortune teller did not skip a beat. "Of course," she said soothingly. "It is he who will be the object of this dark person's revenge. You will get in the way to protect him, but be killed in defending him. Only a proper blessing can save you."

"One hundred dollars a day," I said.

"One hundred dollars a day," Madame Flora

echoed, confident that she had closed the deal.

"Can I ask a question?" Lodge interjected.

"Of course," said Madame Flora.

"What does the Justice card mean?" As he asked the question, I caught another faint whiff of crabapple. I watched intently, knowing something was up.

Madame Flora began to reel off a prepackaged speech about the card of Justice, but only made it halfway through the first sentence before she began to stutter and wheeze. Within seconds, she had fainted and fallen out of her chair, unconscious. I leaned over and checked her pulse. "This may not be the lark you wanted, Walter. I think she's dead."

Lodge scoffed. "She wants you to think she's dead, Morgan. It's an old trick she uses whenever she needs to remove herself from an unpleasant situation. She fakes having a fit, faints, and then appears as though dead. Her clients panic and leave; shortly thereafter, she revives and makes herself scarce from the angry public for a few days. It has worked for her every time—until now."

"What are you going to do?" I asked.

"Revive her." He said a few words in Latin, and she sprang back to life as though a drill sergeant had uttered the words: "Attention!"

"You're still here!" she exclaimed mournfully, once she was sufficiently alert to make such an observation.

"Yes," said Lodge sternly. "You were the only one to leave." He handed her a glass of water to help her revive.

"What are you going to do with me?" she asked, cowering. She had lost all of the bluster and bravado she had exhibited just minutes before.

"Absolutely nothing," Lodge said. "You are your own worst enemy. I just want to get the reading I paid for. So, when you have revived, I want you to get back in your chair and tell us what these cards actually mean."

"Why are you torturing me like this?" she complained. "You already know the meaning of the cards. Why should I read them for you?"

"Because I paid you to do so. And, my friend here does not know what they mean."

So she hoisted herself back into her chair, with some help from the two of us. Then she proceeded to give us a genuine reading, with an occasional prod from Lodge. I learned that the High Priestess represented another fortune teller in our city, a woman who circulated in the highest levels of society and held "teas" at which she would read the fortunes of other women. Madame Flora and Lodge both referred to her as "The Vixen." They also both confirmed that she had likely been the reason behind more than one death over the years, although no crime had ever been traced back to her.

"The eight of swords indicates that she has been trapped in her own web at last," Madame Flora continued, as Lodge nodded agreement. She then looked him directly in the eye and said: "You are the Hermit. You have been searching for the Truth for many centuries, and now you have found it." He smiled thinly and responded with his usual signature, crabapple.

"The Tower indicates a grave tragedy in the past, with many people dying. I do not know how far in the past, but it must have been a long time. The ten of swords lies in the future, but its precise meaning is not clear to me. It is veiled in uncertainty, although I am beginning to sense that the future has already arrived.

She gasped, then looked at Lodge. "Is the Vixen already dead?"

I could tell that the suggestion clicked solidly in Lodge's mind.

"Let's go find out," he ordered.

We adjourned from the scarlet den of blackmail and drove together to the home of the Vixen, in one of the fanciest high rises in town. When we arrived, we found the building cordoned off by the police. I caught the attention of one of the policemen and told him we were expected by the mayor. He let us pass, adding the important words: "eighth floor."

When we arrived, we were greeted by Jack Steele, the mayor, and Adam Goodman, the chief of police. "Why are you here, Lodge?" Jack asked. "I didn't call for you. In fact, we just arrived ourselves."

"Sometimes, I am called by an even higher authority." Lodge replied grimly. "I take it we are too late?"

The mayor let us pass. Inside the apartment, there was a dead corpse, all that remained of the woman who had been the Vixen. There were ten daggers plunged into her back, each one different than the others, each one quite elaborate, even ornate.

"Jeez!" whistled Lodge. "There must be a half million dollars of antiquity plunged in her back. The Vixen died as the most expensive pincushion in history."

"The Vixen?" asked Jack. "Did you know this woman, Lodge?"

"In this lifetime, only by reputation," Lodge asserted. "I did not move in her circles of society."

"Well, what do you make of the crime?" asked Chief Goodman.

Lodge paused for a minute, exploring a

number of possibilities. "She died here," he said. "The body has not been moved or even rearranged." He paused again.

"She was killed by committee, although not by agreement. Each of the ten people who plunged a dagger in her back arrived separately, without any knowledge of what had already happened. The first person came this morning about ten. She was well known to The Vixen—in fact, a client—who let her in. When The Vixen's back was turned, the visitor stabbed her with the dagger she had concealed in her purse. She stabbed just once. Then, awakening to the horror of what she had done, she fled the scene, leaving the door to the apartment ajar—and the knife still fixed in the Vixen's blood-soaked back.

"The second assassin arrived minutes later, with much the same intent. She found the Vixen still alive, although bleeding profusely. She stabbed her again, also leaving her calling card. Incredibly, this same scene was reenacted eight more times, each by a different woman, before her body was discovered by the concierge, who then called you fellows.

"Of course, the Vixen was very much dead before the tenth blow was delivered."

"Are there prints on the daggers?"

"No," replied Lodge. "Each of the women

wore white gloves, as is customary at that level of society. You will be unable to trace them, even if you wanted to do so."

"Why wouldn't I want to trace them?" asked Jack.

"Too much embarrassment for too many important people in this town," Lodge responded. "Besides, even if you did identify these women, you would have a hard time finding a jury that would convict any of them. The Vixen had been blackmailing each of the twelve. She was doing, on a very refined scale, what our friend here, Madame Flora, has been doing on a lesser scale: finding out people's secrets through the guise of foretelling their futures, then using this information to blackmail them.

"The Vixen specialized in providing spells and potions to help these ladies seduce very desirable lovers and have extramarital affairs with them, then turned the tables and used her knowledge of these affairs to blackmail them—often to the tune of a million dollars or more per affair. It was her way of supporting this extravagant lifestyle.

"If you start indicting these ten ladies, Jack, the whole sordid truth will start to tumble out. It will be an avalanche that you cannot stop once it begins." He took the mayor aside and whispered, "Suffice it to say that even you will be drawn into the scandal, if you pursue it."

Jack's face blanched white, as Lodge projected into his awareness a brief glimpse of one of his own daughters consulting The Vixen. He also focused the mayor's attention briefly on one of the ten daggers—long enough for Jack to recognize that the dagger had belonged to him. He had given it to his daughter, now in her twenties, the year before for Christmas, knowing that she had always admired it.

Jack quickly regained his self-control, however, and his color returned. He looked at the chief of police. "Ten daggers in the back," he said shaking his head; "what a horrible way to commit suicide."

Chief Goodman ordered the daggers removed and "preserved for evidence." Years later, a set of nine daggers—minus the one that belonged to Jack—was quietly donated to the city museum, where they became one of the most spectacular exhibits in the entire United States.

We parted company and went back to our car to drive Madame Flora back to her modest storefront.

"I don't know," I said with some bewilderment. "I don't think that we uncovered the whole story."

"We didn't," Lodge laughed. "We only read the first six cards of the Tarot spread. We left four cards unread—deliberately. They are the cards that tell the truth. Would you like to finish the reading, Madame Flora, or shall I?"

"Be my guest," replied the fortune teller. "I can tell when I have been outclassed."

"The last four cards, from the bottom up, are Justice, the Magician, Judgment, and the ten of swords. The card of Justice indicates that the events of today can only be fully understood in the context of the events of years gone by. In the seventeenth century, the Vixen lived in Paris and was known as *La Voison*. She was a fortune teller and a practitioner of witchcraft. She became very popular in the highest reaches of French society, providing potions and spells so that her clients could seduce anyone they set their eye on. It was only after an investigator spent three years pursuing *La Voison* that the scandal broke—but when it broke, it broke big. It was revealed that one of *La Voison's* clients was mistress to the king—Louis the XIV—and had in fact used *La Voison's* spells and philtres to win the favor of the king. Naturally, the king did not like this news, and ordered the investigation halted. In spite of this, *La Voison* and some thirty of her clients were burned at the stake for witchcraft.

"Many of the women who were burned were not actually guilty of anything more than gullibility—a stunning lack of Judgment, as suggested by the third card in the final column. I think we would find that the ten women who executed The Vixen today were probably enacting a very effective ritual of revenge.

"But what about the Magician and the ten of swords?" I asked.

"Need I explain everything?" Lodge retorted with a sigh. "The Magician in this case is divine justice itself, which arranged to have these ten women converge on this apartment at precise intervals on this fateful day, and add their vote to the death sentence on The Vixen. The events were arranged with incredible detail, down to the fact that each woman used a dagger from the time of Louis XIV. Did you see some of those dirks? Some of them had a king's ransom of jewels encrusted in their handles. Each has a history of mystery wrapped up within it—and now a new chapter has been added. It took some twenty years for these women to come into possession of these daggers; divine justice can be exceedingly patient, don't you think? The ten of swords indicates, quite literally, the ten daggers plunged in *La Voison's* back. Under the circumstances, I think Jack's ruling of suicide was the correct decision. The Vixen brought on this tragedy through her own schemes."

"You have lost us again, Lodge," I complained. "What do you mean by that?"

"The Vixen had told each of these ten women that if they brought her a dagger from the time of Louis XIV, she would cast a spell of protection around it—for a small consideration of course. In this case, the small consideration was $10,000 a dagger. The enchanted dagger would then protect each of the ladies from all potential danger.

"The only flaw in her thinking was that she failed to realize that she was the principal danger to her court of ten. So, once all ten daggers had been collected and enchanted, the daggers actually put the spell to work. They generated a vortex in fate that led directly to her own murder.

"So, you see—it was suicide!"

We had arrived at the consulting rooms of Madame Flora. "I am neither blind nor deaf," she announced as she got out of our car. "I am going to retire from fortune telling." Then she disappeared inside.

"I hope she keeps her promise," Lodge said, as we pulled away. "But I suspect she will just move to a different city and start in again. She may even try to operate at the level of The

Vixen, but she does not have what it takes."

"I have just three questions left," I said.

"What are they?" asked Lodge.

"First, why did Madame Flora try to pull a bunk by fainting?"

Lodge smiled. "When I asked her to interpret Justice, the card acted somewhat like a mirror—not because she was implicated in the crime, but because she mirrored The Vixen in so many ways. She did not like what she saw, and tried to run away from it. That moment opened up intuitive senses which she never had before. Now we shall see if she can use them responsibly."

"That makes sense. Next question: I thought the Tarot reading was supposed to be for me. It certainly turned out to be accurate enough, but I hardly think it applies to me."

"I suppose you are right," said Lodge. "But I do not remember promising to have your future in particular foretold—just the future in general. You certainly cannot dispute that the future was foretold."

"Quite true. But that brings up a corollary question. Is the Tarot genuine, or is it nonsense?"

"You saw it in both lights today, didn't you?" Lodge smiled. "In the hands of a gypsy fortune teller, it is nonsense—a tool for depriving honest but gullible people of their money.

But in the hands of a trained intuitive, it can be a wonderful tool, not just for predicting the future but for understanding all of the intricacies of any problem or situation." He turned. "And your other question?"

"Why were you drawn into this sordid mess?"

Lodge chuckled. "Why? Why indeed? Why do I ever use my intuitive skills to solve crimes? I guess it is in my blood, as well as in my mind.

"In 1679, I was Nicolas de la Reynie, the investigator who uncovered and prosecuted the scandal of *La Voisin*. It was my right to be in on the final episode of that scandal, even though I was not directly involved in it.

"Today, I exercised that right."

Fourteen

The Needle In the Haystack

I had not sipped my first cup of coffee when Lodge, sitting at the breakfast table, boldly declared: "Ah, Morgan! Today is the day Jack will be elected governor of the state."

Even without coffee, I realized that it was not the first Tuesday in November. No elections were being held—and even if they were, Jack was not running for governor, let alone campaigning. This worried me, for Lodge always spoke precisely. He was not given to hyperbole.

"Does Jack know this?" I managed to mumble.

"Of course not," Lodge laughed heartily. "Neither do the good people of the state. But mark my words: Jack will win the election today, even though the actual race is still more than a year away."

"Your words are duly marked," I replied. "Do we tell Jack—or keep this our own little secret?"

"Oh, we keep it a secret," answered Lodge. "He'll find out soon enough. In fact, he will be joining us for breakfast. I called him an hour ago to invite him. He had some kind of fund raising breakfast on his schedule, but he canceled it when I mentioned that hundreds of thousands of lives could be at stake—including his—if he did not come over."

Lodge let that teaser dangle in the room until Jack arrived. I allowed it to hang as well, keeping myself busy with eggs and bacon and toast. I knew from experience that once Jack showed up, I would learn what I needed to know—and my chances of finishing breakfast would drop to near zero. So I made sure I ate what I could.

The mayor appeared a few minutes later, accepted Mrs. Milledge's offer of orange juice and a soft-boiled egg, and then asked Lodge: "Now, what is so important that I had to forfeit the pleasure of breakfasting with one hundred old men to come over here?"

"The Needle," Lodge replied, as though those two words explained everything.

The Needle was a common nickname for the tallest skyscraper in the city—a building that has dominated the skyline for more than fifty years.

"The Needle!" Jack exclaimed. "That's just where I came from. My breakfast meeting was being held at the Drake." The Hotel Drake occupies a large part of the lower levels of the Needle, as well as the upper three floors, where its restaurant—and penthouse suites—are located.

"There is a plot in progress to blow the Needle to very small bits later this morning," Lodge announced.

Jack dropped his spoon. "What?"

"It is to be blown up with explosives quite similar to the ones used in Oklahoma City. In this case, however, the Needle is being targeted for the express purpose of trying to inflict as much damage on the entire downtown area as possible. The plotters hope that debris will be hurled as far as a half mile away by the force of the explosion. This is why they selected the Needle as a target. It is not really a target as much as it is a weapon itself. They anticipate that the exploding building will become millions of projectiles wreaking havoc over a very widespread area."

"Are they right?" Jack inquired.

"I am not a munitions expert," Lodge responded, "but it strikes me as a very serious threat. The lower floors of the Needle are made of a lot of glass. Flying glass and the explosion itself would do great damage in the immediate area. They also have one of their team already inside the building. He has rigged a set of minor explosives to blow the top of the building in as many directions as possible. These smaller devices are set to be detonated when the major explosive goes off. They are all triggered by the same remote."

"When is this supposed to happen?" asked the mayor.

"In about two hours, at nine thirty," Lodge continued. "The time was chosen to maximize the number of deaths, both in the Needle and in the area beyond."

"Who are the plotters?"

"That is a more difficult question to answer," Lodge replied. "As far as I can tell, they are not residents of the city. They are not even presently here in the city. They are driving a truck loaded with explosives from somewhere out of town. At the moment, they are about an hour away."

"How do you know all this?" asked Jack.

"I have a skill I call 'far seeing' that I picked up thousands of years ago in Egypt. Some of the early Pharaohs used clairvoyants to scan the borders mentally every day, looking for signs of invasion from neighboring countries. It was a means of defense first developed in Atlantis. When alerted to danger, Pharaoh would dispatch a troop of soldiers to ambush the invading forces—under the guidance of the far seers, of course. I was one of these seers many lifetimes ago. I helped defeat two invasions by Babylonians.

"When I awoke this morning, I had a pounding headache—a condition I experience only rarely. I have learned over the years that such headaches are always a sign of psychic malice. It wasn't too hard to focus in on this nefarious plot. Suffice it to say, the hatred and vileness in the minds and hearts of the terrorists are quite intense. They are ready to die in order to inflict mass destruction upon the city. Their projected thoughts are certainly strong enough to give me a nauseating headache!"

"Do you need some aspirin?" asked Jack solicitously.

Lodge laughed. "Aspirin may be a wonder drug, but it provides absolutely no relief from terrorism! I have my own methods of overcoming headaches—I feel fine now, thank you—but the terrorists are still intent upon murder and mayhem."

"Why are they picking on us? Why didn't they choose to blow up Washington—or New York?" Jack was showing signs of panicking. By focusing on Lodge's description, he seemed to be tuning into the terrorists a bit too much for his own good.

Lodge looked into Jack's eyes. "They

thought about blowing up the Washington Monument, but rejected it because it stands by itself. It might well explode without causing the kind of ancillary damage they are hoping will occur. Of all the possible targets, they considered the Needle the best choice for maximum damage. This is why they are heading our way, even as we speak." He paused for a moment, then added:

"But there is another, far more important reason—one unknown to them—why they chose this city."

"What?" asked Jack.

"Because you are its mayor," Lodge said.

"They have something against me?"

"No, no, no!" cried Lodge. "Quite the contrary. They have no idea who you are. But you are the only sitting mayor who has the ability to stop them. They were 'encouraged' to choose our city as their target in order to thwart their intentions."

"Encouraged by whom?" asked Jack.

"By certain invisible forces that do not wish to see this happen," Lodge answered. "Now, I suggest we stop speculating on why and why not, and get busy taking action to prevent a catastrophe."

The mayor sat quite still for about thirty seconds, absorbing the shock of what he had just been told. His city—his responsibility—was under seige from a group of malcontents, driving toward downtown in a loaded truck, ready to commit suicide, if necessary, to inflict terror on thousands of unsuspecting citizens and destroy most of the downtown area. It was almost more than any human being could contemplate—and now he was being given the duty to prevent it. In one sense, nothing in his training had prepared him for this moment. And yet, in another sense, *everything* in his training had made him ready for this moment.

In the space of that thirty seconds of silence, Jack transformed himself from a man on the verge of panic to a calm, determined, fearless man of action. When he looked up at Lodge again, he was ready to move decisively.

"May I set up my command headquarters here in your kitchen? I do not think there is time to return to City Hall."

"It would be my honor, Your Honor," Lodge said with a slight smile. He had counted on Jack rising to the occasion, and was glad to see his faith in the mayor rewarded.

"Do you have any idea from what direction these goons are approaching the city?" Jack asked.

"They are presently fifty miles east of the city limits on the interstate," Lodge replied.

"Then let's tear a page from your experiences in Egypt," Jack said, "and lure them into an ambush. Our first step should be to misdirect them away from downtown, so that if the truck explodes, it will do less harm. Do we have time to throw up a roadblock?"

"A roadblock may not be the best solution," Lodge suggested. "They will just crash through it—and it will tip them off that we know what they are doing."

"Then how about a different kind of diversion?" Jack did not even wait for an answer. He picked up the phone and called the city's highway department, ordering a crew to erect a series of temporary signs on the interstate, just outside the city. "Put every man you have on this job," he ordered. "Get it done—now!"

The first sign announced "Bridge Out." It was to be accompanied by all of the orange cones and barricades the crew could muster, funneling all traffic into one lane and then down the next exit.

The second sign, at the exit, ordered: "Detour: Follow Route 305."

Route 305, of course, went nowhere near downtown. It led, without any crossroads, straight to the city dump—a fact that only lifelong residents of the immediate area would probably know.

"I'm counting on the terrorists not being familiar with the geography around our city," said Jack as he hung up.

"You are probably in luck," Lodge replied. "They spent a lot of time studying the Needle—but didn't think of making contingencies for detours thirty miles out of town. This scheme may just work. But how are you keeping all of the other interstate traffic from heading to the dump as well?"

Jack beamed. "I have instructed the crew to position the orange barrels so that the traffic can be funneled one of two ways. Ordinary traffic will be directed down Route 440—which rejoins the interstate in about four miles.

"Route 440 would be the logical detour, of course. My plan counts on being able to spot the truck before it reaches the barrels. When the spotters see it, they will warn the rest of the crew by walkie-talkie, and the barrels will be quickly repositioned to send the truck down Route 305—directly toward the dump.

"In case other vehicles follow before we can switch the barrels back, we will try our best to keep them out of harm's way. But we are hoping the flow of traffic will not pose any such problems.

"Speaking of that, is it possible to give us a description of the truck?"

"It is a twenty-eight-foot long straight truck painted green and white. It was stolen three days ago from the Harland Nursery, and its logo says: 'We make green things grow.' The word 'grow' has been crossed out by one of the terrorists, who inserted the word 'blow' in its place. It has a North Carolina license plate. The first three numerals are 879. I cannot make out the rest."

Jack passed the information along to the state police, who set up plainclothes observers to locate and trace the progress of the invading terrorists. He alerted local hospitals, and had several fire departments converge on the city dump. He also ordered the evacuation of the Needle and all surrounding buildings downtown, cordoning off the whole block.

As an after-thought, he asked one of his aides to call the major media and invite them to join the city in a "major emergency tune-up exercise" being conducted at the dump. Since the media was being specifically invited, they assumed the exercises were unimportant, and made only a perfunctory effort to respond. Had they known of the terrorist threat, hundreds of reporters and camera men would have descended on the dump. Instead, only three reporters and two photographers put in an appearance—exactly what Jack wanted. "Now I cannot be accused of failing to keep the media informed," Jack smiled.

After about twenty minutes of hectic telephoning, in which Jack laid down every precaution imaginable, a helicopter landed in the side yard of Lodge's estate. As this was not a normal occurrence, even Lodge was a bit surprised. "We've done just about everything we can from here," said Jack. "This is our ticket to the dump."

We all clambered aboard and were soon circling above the city, preparing to make the five-minute flight. But Lodge seemed troubled.

"The idea of the ambush is a great one, and you have been masterful in mobilizing your forces so quickly," he said, "but something is not going right. Give me a few minutes to think." In a flash, Lodge was no longer with us. His body was still there, strapped into his seat, but the rest of him was elsewhere. Once again, he was searching for a needle in a haystack.

I wish I could describe adequately what was happening inside Lodge's mind. Over the years, Lodge has taught me to better utilize my own mental powers, but I am still a rookie compared to him. It is hard to describe the intuitive state of mind to someone who has not yet experienced it. Basically, the mind expands to encompass the field of investigation. In this instance, Lodge was focusing his tremendous powers of concentration on the threat posed by these terrorists, thereby connecting him with all relevant information. Through this act of concentration, he drew this relevant information into his awareness. He plucked the needle not just from the haystack, but from the entire hayloft—and, indeed, all surrounding haylofts!

He came back to us just before we landed. "The moment you ordered the evacuation of downtown, the terrorist who had been stationed ahead of time in the Needle was on a cell phone relaying the news. Apparently, they had two trucks all along. In addition to the stolen nursery van, there is another truck five miles behind it. It seems to be the one carrying the explosives. The plan is to let the nursery truck lead the way and take whatever heat we give them, but keep the real truck heading to its intended target."

Jack groaned—but only for a moment. A sly smile flashed across his face, and he reached for his cell phone. Punching in the necessary numbers, he waited for a response, then barked a few short orders into the receiver and hung up. He turned to us and reported: "I have asked the FBI to position a car between the two trucks and intercept the cellular signal. They will prevent the signals broadcast by the nursery truck from getting to the explosives truck, and then substitute whatever misinformation will lead the terrorists to the city dump."

We touched down on the edge of the dump, then jogged across to where the police had set up a temporary command center. Lodge followed at a sedate saunter.

The city dump was a controlled land fill project covering hundreds of acres. The genius Jack had exhibited in choosing this location became clear: the land fill formed a natural ampitheater, which let the police and other city officials encircle it. There was just one road into the giant circle—and only one road out. It was a one-lane, dirt track.

Jack had ordered the fire department to hose down the center of the pit, right at the end of the dirt road. An area about the size of half a football field was rapidly becoming a muddy morass.

Adam Goodman, the chief of police, was the first to greet us. "What are we dealing with here?" he asked Jack. Jack had taken special care not to divulge too much information to anyone, lest it be intercepted by the terrorists.

"A terrorist plot to blow up downtown," he barked back.

"Then why are we at the city dump?" asked Goodman.

"We're trying to draw them over here instead," was Jack's only answer.

The chief was not satisfied. "What if they crash the 'bridge out' sign and keep heading for downtown?"

"I have the air force standing by, ready to blow 'em to hell," Jack replied. "They would be the only ones on the road; they would be an easy target. But I would just as soon not blow up ten million bucks worth of interstate."

That was when Lodge caught up with the rest of us. "I would urge you to try to capture them without gunfire," he said. "A stray bullet could easily blow up the truck."

"My thoughts exactly," said Jack. "In fact, I want the dump cleared of everyone who is not essential. I do not want anyone hurt, let alone killed, if we can avoid it."

An update came in from the FBI. The nursery van had turned off the interstate and was heading toward the dump. The unmarked FBI car travelling between the two trucks was busy feeding false information to the terrorists, spinning a story about "outguessing the cops."

The mayor's plan was a simple one. He would wait until the second truck was almost to the dump, then hem in the terrorists from behind, forcing them to drive the truck into the dump. Once surrounded, he hoped they would surrender without gunfire.

"Just remember, Jack—they are terrorists," Lodge advised. "They were willing to die today if they had to detonate the truck before getting out of harm's way. So don't expect them to surrender, even if it's a rational option. They have no scruples about taking human life—even their own."

"Are you trying to warn me about something I do not know?" Jack replied.

"Let me just say that I do not anticipate any of the terrorists being alive very much longer," Lodge said quietly. "They seem to have signed some kind of suicide pact. Even the fellow already at the Needle will probably kill himself if the plot goes awry."

"What motivates goons like this?" the mayor asked.

"It's a phenomenon society does not understand at all," Lodge said. "We tend to regard these people as political protestors. Some people actually admire them. But they use political and social causes only to mask their true motive—which is to create mayhem.

They are professional trouble makers. Their only god is chaos. They hate order. When you look at their past lives, they tend to come from countries which still embrace terrorism—countries with a long tradition of terrorism.

"It is always a mistake to try to deal rationally with terrorism. It must be met directly and forcefully. Society must never give in. We must never believe that a little bit of terrorism is no big deal. A little bit of terrorism would have blown up the entire downtown commercial center today, if we had not intervened."

At that point, Jack was advised by the FBI that the second truck had turned off the interstate and was heading our way. They estimated that we would see the truck in about two minutes—and then almost immediately afterward, we would see their back-door route sealed off.

By this time, the stolen nursery truck had arrived in our midst. It rolled slowly into the middle of the circle, coming to a stop in the mud. The driver tried to drive out of it, but could not. His wheels spun vainly in the mud. He became frustrated, then started gunning his engine. The wheels spun more furiously. But all he managed to do was slide the truck sideways. There they sat, immobilized by mud.

It is impossible to know exactly what the

terrorists did in the last minute or so of their lives. They had been confident that they could draw the fire of the police forces massed against them, and let the second truck proceed unmolested to their target destination. It must have been devastating to them to see the second truck drive over the rim of the dump, rolling straight at them—with about forty police cars following at a safe distance behind.

Lodge suddenly realized what was happening. "My God, Jack—tell the police cars to stop. Now!" Jack relayed the command to the police, and the entire caravan suddenly came to a thunderous halt.

The next few seconds unfolded as if in slow motion. The second truck accelerated, trying to ram into the first. But once it hit the mud, the truck spun violently out of control, capsizing. It had failed to strike the other truck. It just lay there, like a wounded behemoth.

One second later, the two trucks exploded in unison, spewing a pillar of fire and concussion hundreds of feet in the air. Apparently the terrorists had chosen to detonate—and both trucks had been loaded with explosives!

Even though we were hundreds of yards away from the impact, we hit the deck. We could feel the terrible draft of hot air rush by us, then subside. We let a good number of moments pass before Lodge cautiously stood up. The rest of us followed his lead. There was only a large crater where the two trucks had become stuck in the mud moments before. The rest of the scene resembled a recently scorched war zone.

"Imagine what damage this would have done downtown," said Adam.

"I do not need to imagine," said Jack. "This is bad enough."

Lodge turned to the mayor. "You had better get an explosives team into the Needle right away, to find and disarm the explosive devices they had already planted. I do not think they can be detonated now that these two trucks have been blown up, but there is no point taking chances. Just remember—there is still one man at large."

That one man was found hours later—in little pieces in the Needle's underground garage. When he realized his comrades had died, he detonated a small bomb he had strapped to himself. It was large enough to kill him, but did no structural damage to the garage.

In spite of the fact that both trucks had been loaded with explosives, not a single participant in the drama had been hurt—other than the terrorists. The city did lose about twenty police cars, however—all of them in the first line of pursuit. The cars protected their passengers and drivers, but the intense heat damaged them beyond repair.

"That was close," said Jack.

"Too close," agreed Lodge. "The head terrorist formulated his plan to crash into his own truck only once he saw that he was trapped. It was his intent to take with him as many of the police as he could. He made his decision so late in the chase that I had only a split second to register it and pass the word along."

He turned to Jack. "This city is lucky you acted so fearlessly today. You saved thousands of lives and billions of dollars."

Jack demurred. "It was you who deserve our thanks, Lodge."

Lodge smiled. "Me? I wasn't even here. Any impression you have to the contrary is just all in your mind." And he walked back toward the helicopter.

The next day, the morning paper ran a huge photograph of the scene, under the headline: "Mayor Saves City." The picture, taken at the moment of impact, showed the huge fireball exploding into the sky. It also showed the mayor, with me at his side, just a split second before we hit the ground. We were still standing up, pointing to the trucks. But Lodge was nowhere to be seen in the photograph.

I know for a fact he was still standing at the moment the picture was snapped, because he landed on top of me when we hit the ground. Still, he did not appear in the photograph. It looked, as he said, as though he was not there.

I pointed this out over breakfast. "How did you do that?" I asked.

Lodge smirked. "I rendered myself invisible to the cameras," he admitted.

"I wish you had rendered yourself weightless to your associate," I retorted. Lodge laughed. "Why did you go to all that trouble? You're not afraid of reprisals, certainly?"

"Good heavens, no!" Lodge chortled. "But it was important that this little escapade be Jack's triumph—not mine. Only a few people know the role I play. It is better to keep it that way, and this will be a highly publicized case. Do you remember what I said yesterday?"

"What—about it being the day Jack would be elected governor?"

"Yes. On the whole, the day turned out perfectly. Jack is an instant hero—the man who saved his city. He is a shoo-in to be elected governor. It would be folly for me to allow anything—even a picture of me standing next to him—to jeopardize the course of Fate."

Ordering More Copies

Additional copies of *It's All in The Mind* are available at your favorite bookstore, or directly from the publisher, Enthea Press. To order from the publisher, please send $14.99 for each copy, plus $4 for postage. Send check or money order in U.S. funds to Ariel Press, P.O. Box 297, Marble Hill, GA 30148. Or call toll free at 1-800-336-7769 and charge the order to Master-Card, VISA, Discover, American Express, or Diners. In Georgia, add sales tax. If you prefer, you may fax a credit card order to us at (706) 579-1865.

Be sure to check us out on the internet at http://workoflight.home.att.net.

Other books by Carl Japikse are also available from Enthea Press, as well as at your local bookstore. Selected titles include:

THE HOUR GLASS
A Collection of Fables, $14.95

THE ZEN OF FARTING
The Story of Reepah Gud Wan, $9.99

THE FABLED GATE
The Esoteric Meaning of Mythology, $14.99